JOHNNY BOO
DOES SOMETHING

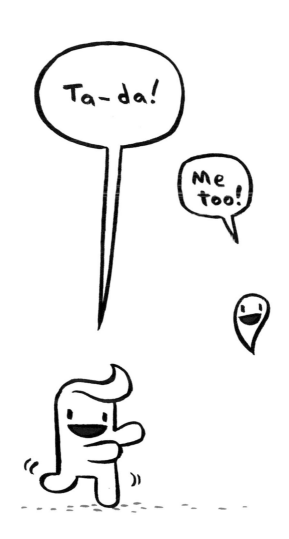

HOW TO READ THIS BOOK:

Read my parts in YOUR Regular voice.

My voice is high and squeaky!

ISBN 978-1-60309-084-1
1. Children's Books
2. Ghosts
3. Graphic Novels

Johnny Boo Does Something! © 2013 James Kochalka. Published by Top Shelf Productions, PO Box 1282, Marietta, GA 30061-1282, USA. Publishers: Brett Warnock and Chris Staros. Top Shelf Productions ® and the Top Shelf logo are registered trademarks of Top Shelf Productions, Inc. All Rights Reserved. No part of this publication may be reproduced without permission, except for small excerpts for purposes of review. Visit our online catalog at www.topshelfcomix.com.

First Printing, March, 2013. Printed in China.

CHAPTER ONE:

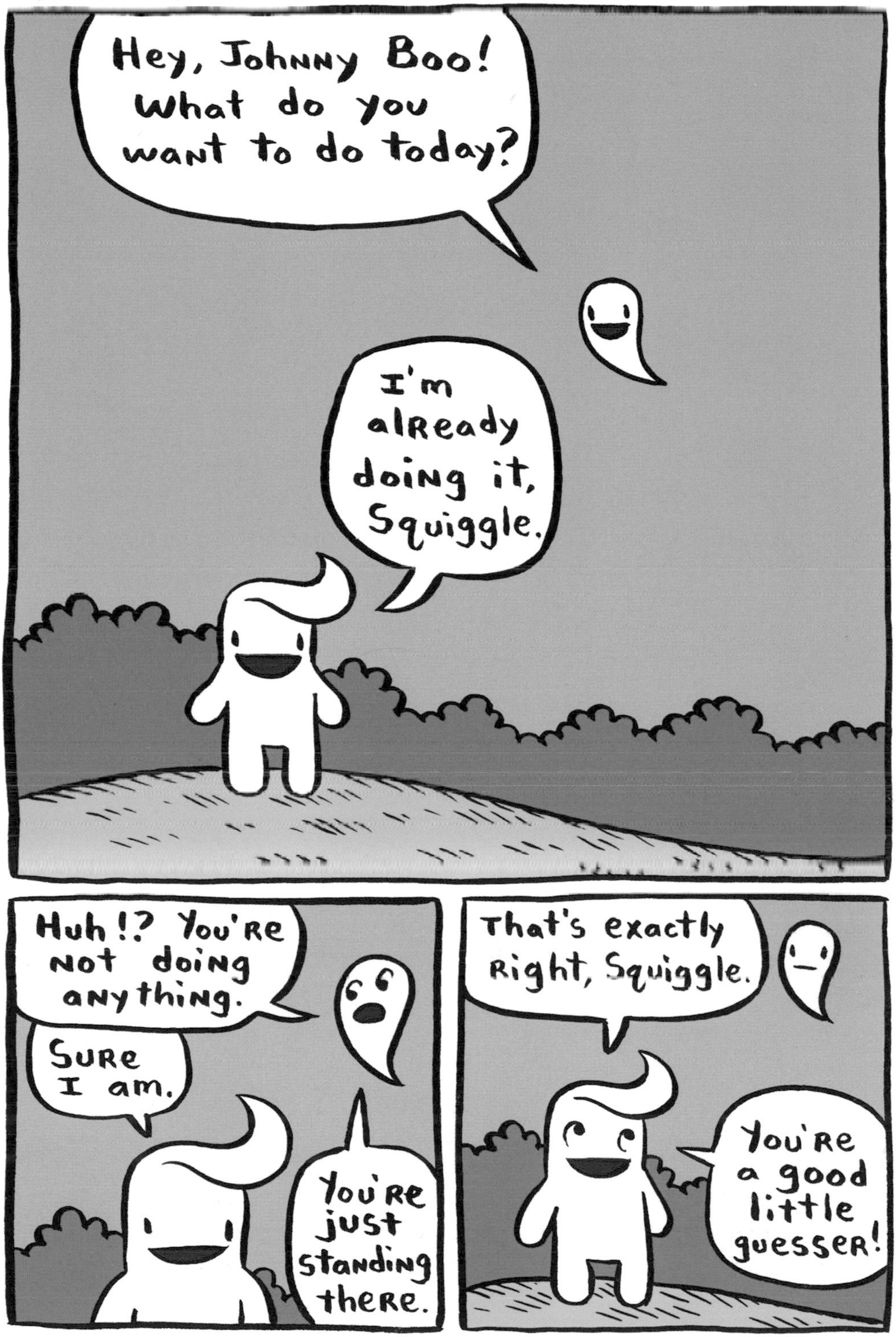
Hey, Johnny Boo! What do you want to do today?
I'm already doing it, Squiggle.
Huh!? You're not doing anything.
Sure I am.
You're just standing there.
That's exactly right, Squiggle.
You're a good little guesser!

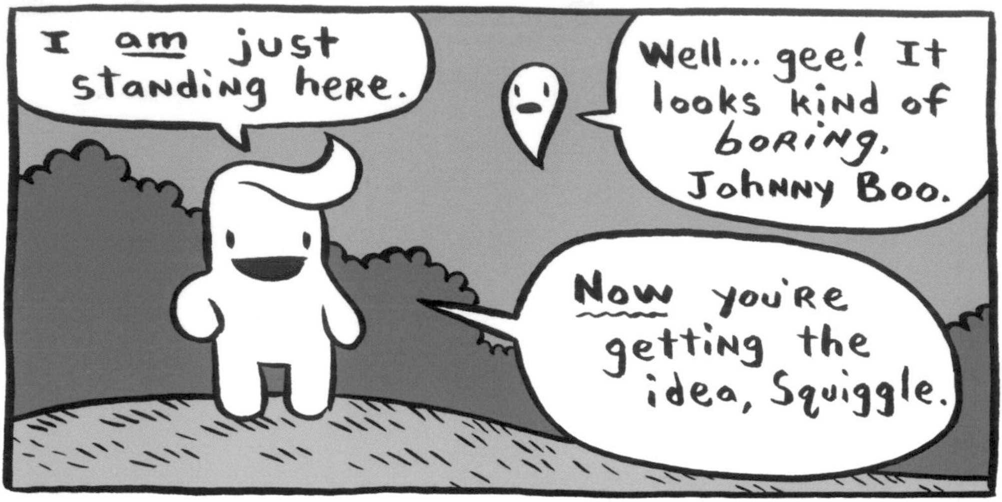
I am just standing here.
Well... gee! It looks kind of boring, Johnny Boo.
Now you're getting the idea, Squiggle.

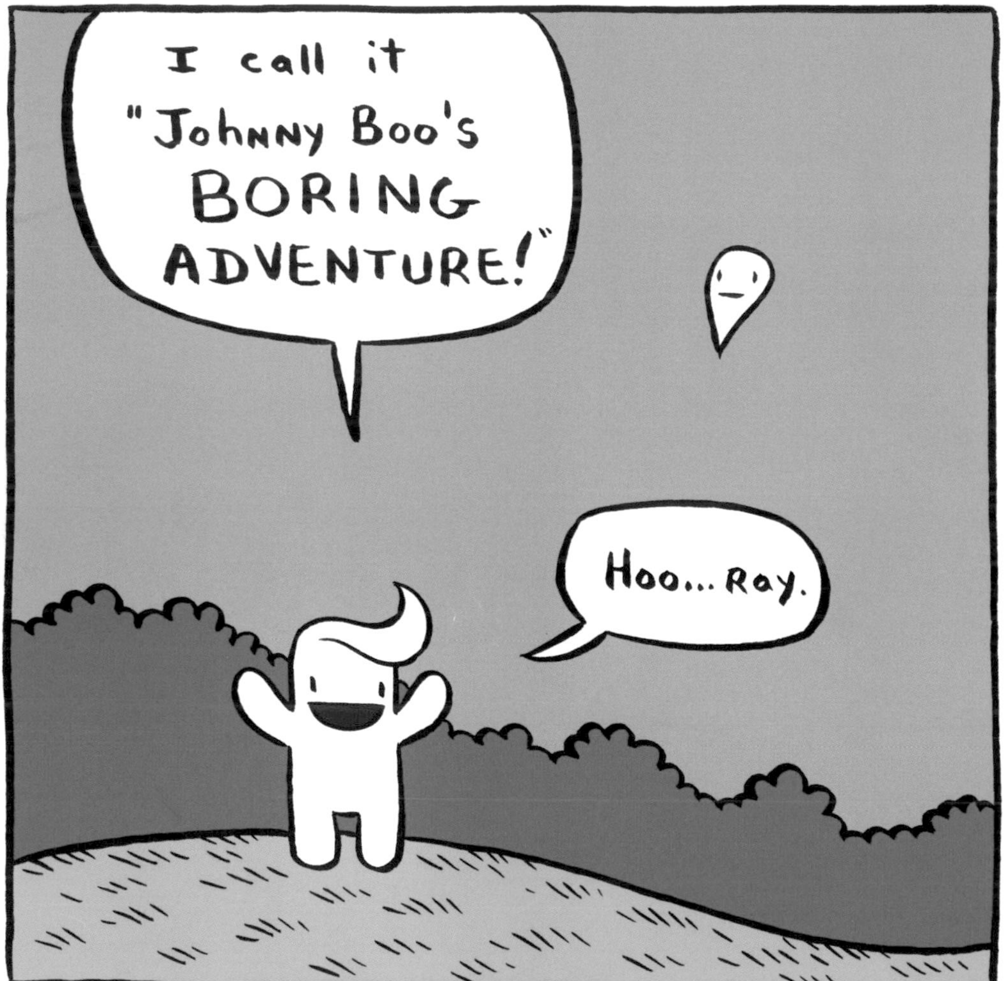
I call it "Johnny Boo's BORING ADVENTURE!"
Hoo... Ray.

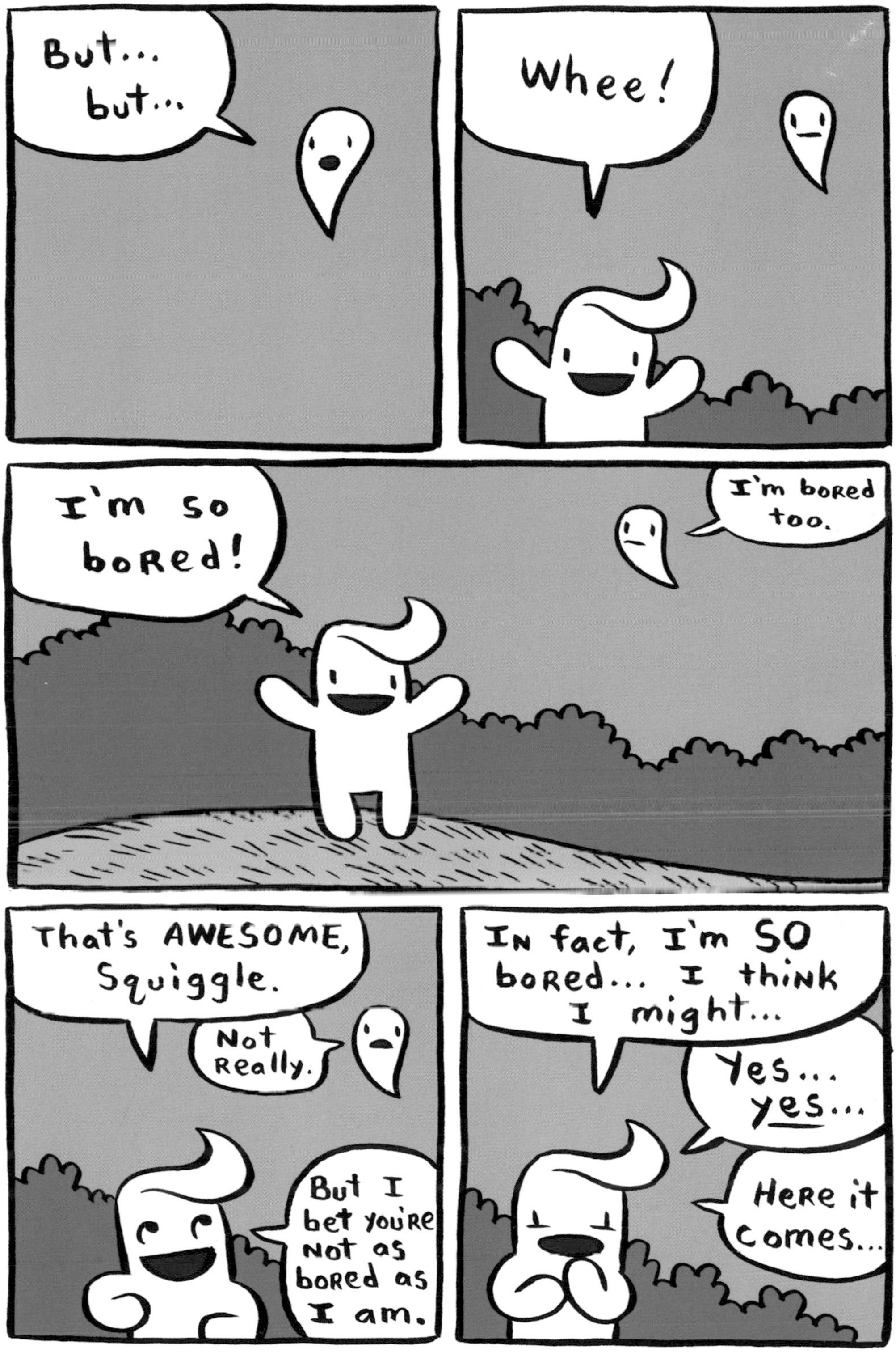
But... but...
Whee!
I'm so bored!
I'm bored too.
That's AWESOME, Squiggle.
Not Really.
But I bet you're not as bored as I am.
In fact, I'm SO bored... I think I might...
Yes... yes...
Here it comes...

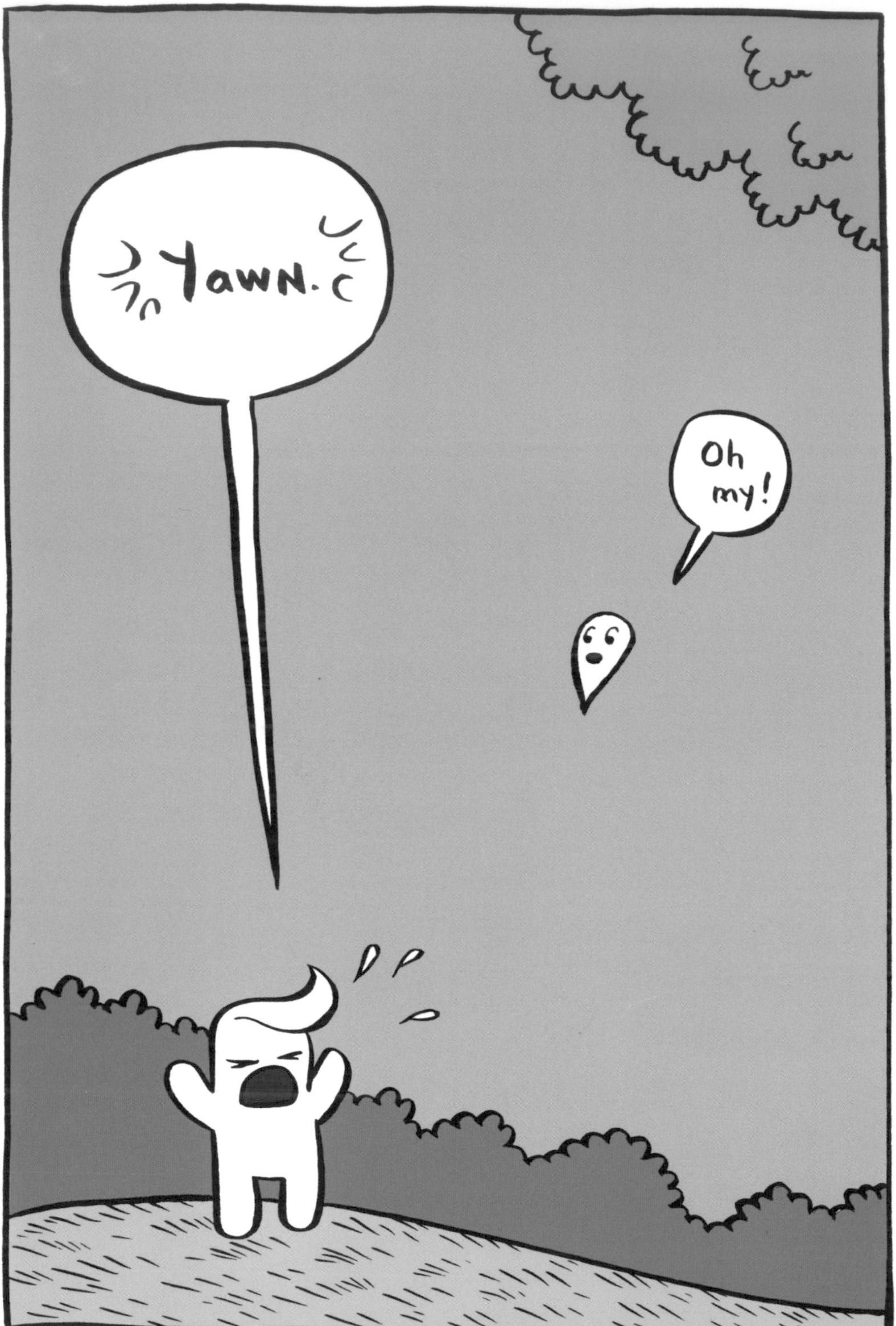
Yawn.
Oh my!

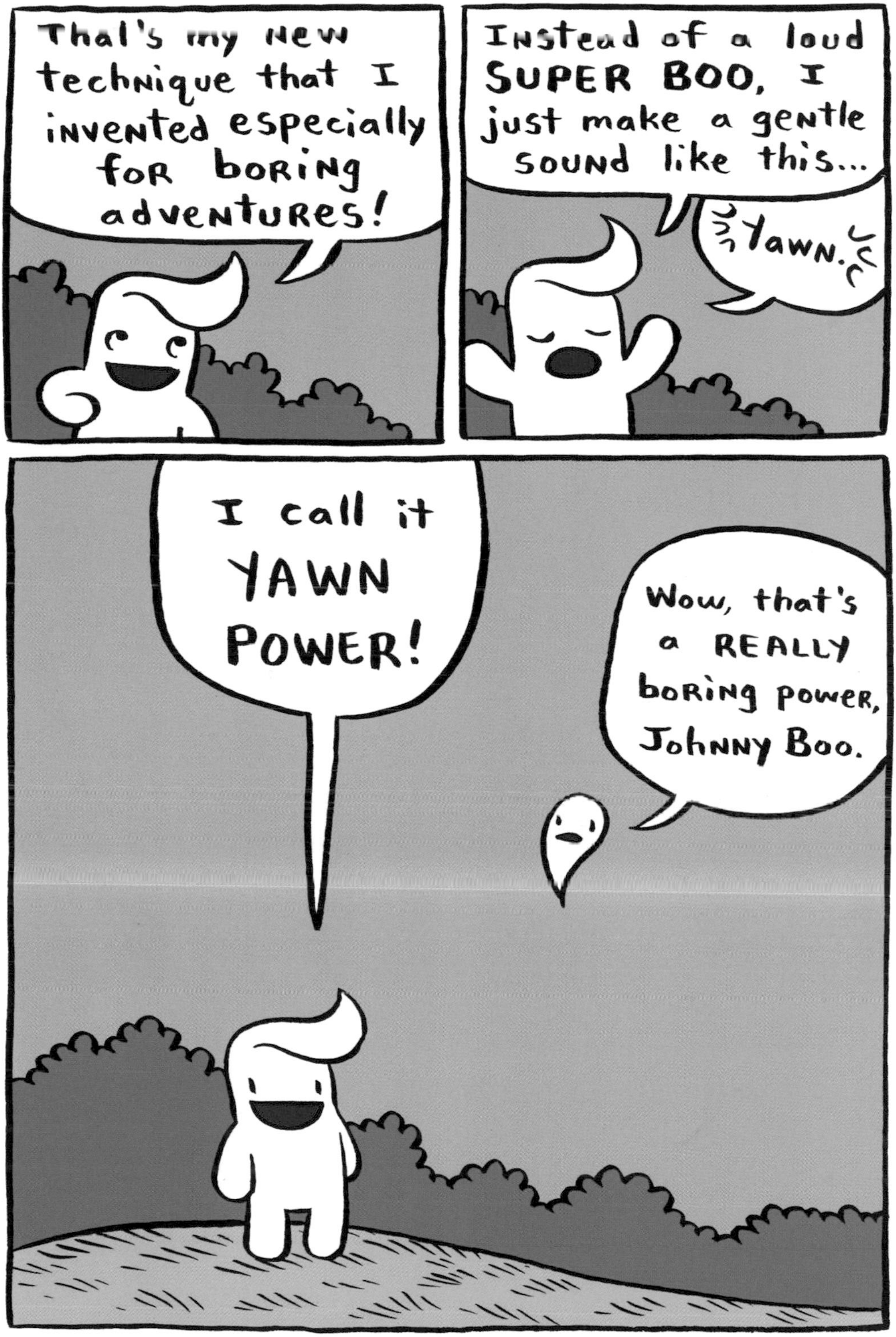
That's my new technique that I invented especially for boring adventures!
Instead of a loud SUPER BOO, I just make a gentle sound like this...
Yawn.
I call it YAWN POWER!
Wow, that's a REALLY boring power, Johnny Boo.

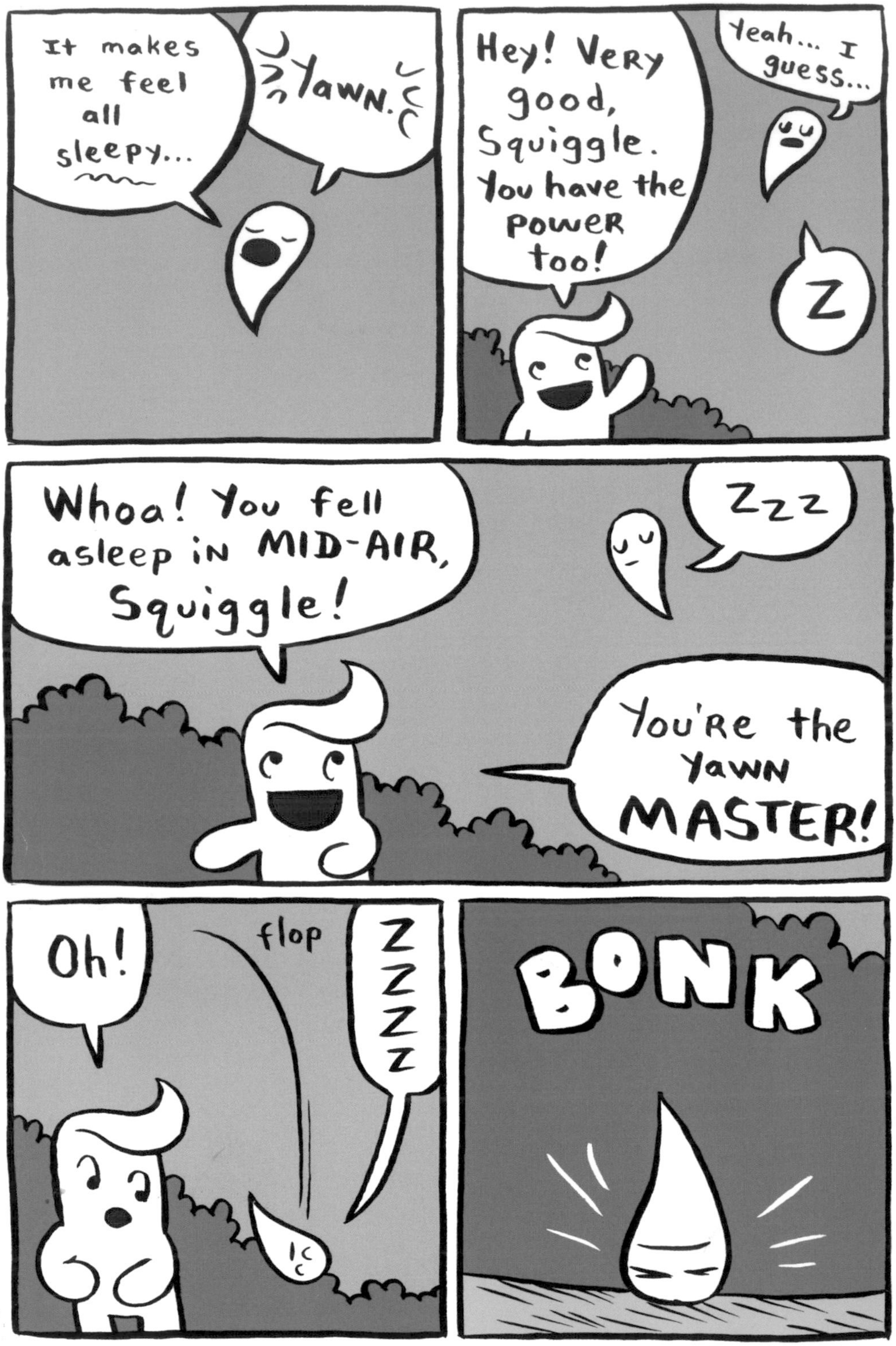
It makes me feel all sleepy...
YAWN.
Hey! VERY good, Squiggle. You have the POWER too!
Yeah... I guess...
Z
Whoa! You fell asleep in MID-AIR, Squiggle!
ZZZ
You're the YAWN MASTER!
Oh!
flop
ZZZZZ
BONK

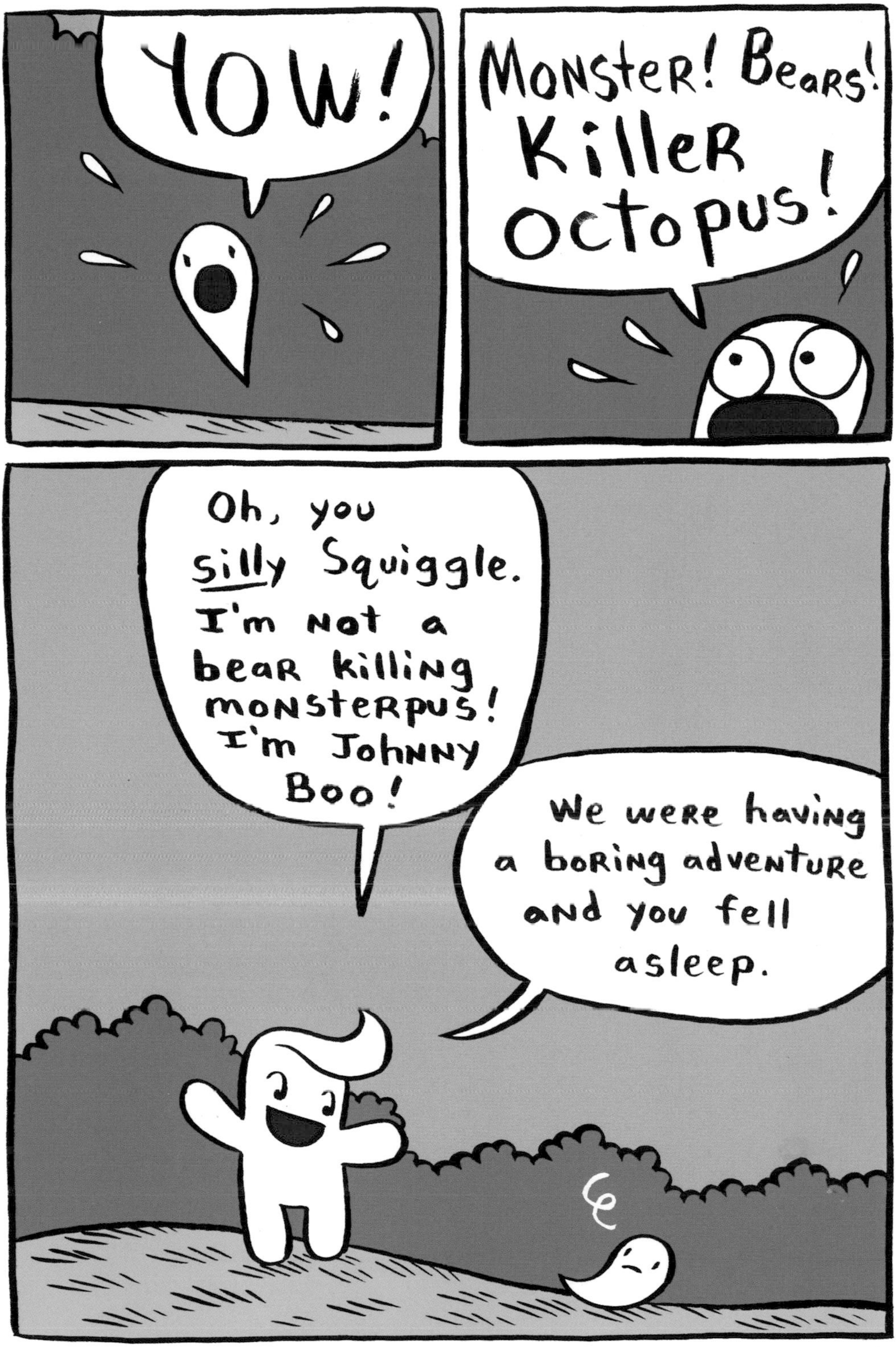
YOW!
Monster! Bears! Killer Octopus!
Oh, you silly Squiggle. I'm not a bear killing monsterpus! I'm Johnny Boo!
We were having a boring adventure and you fell asleep.

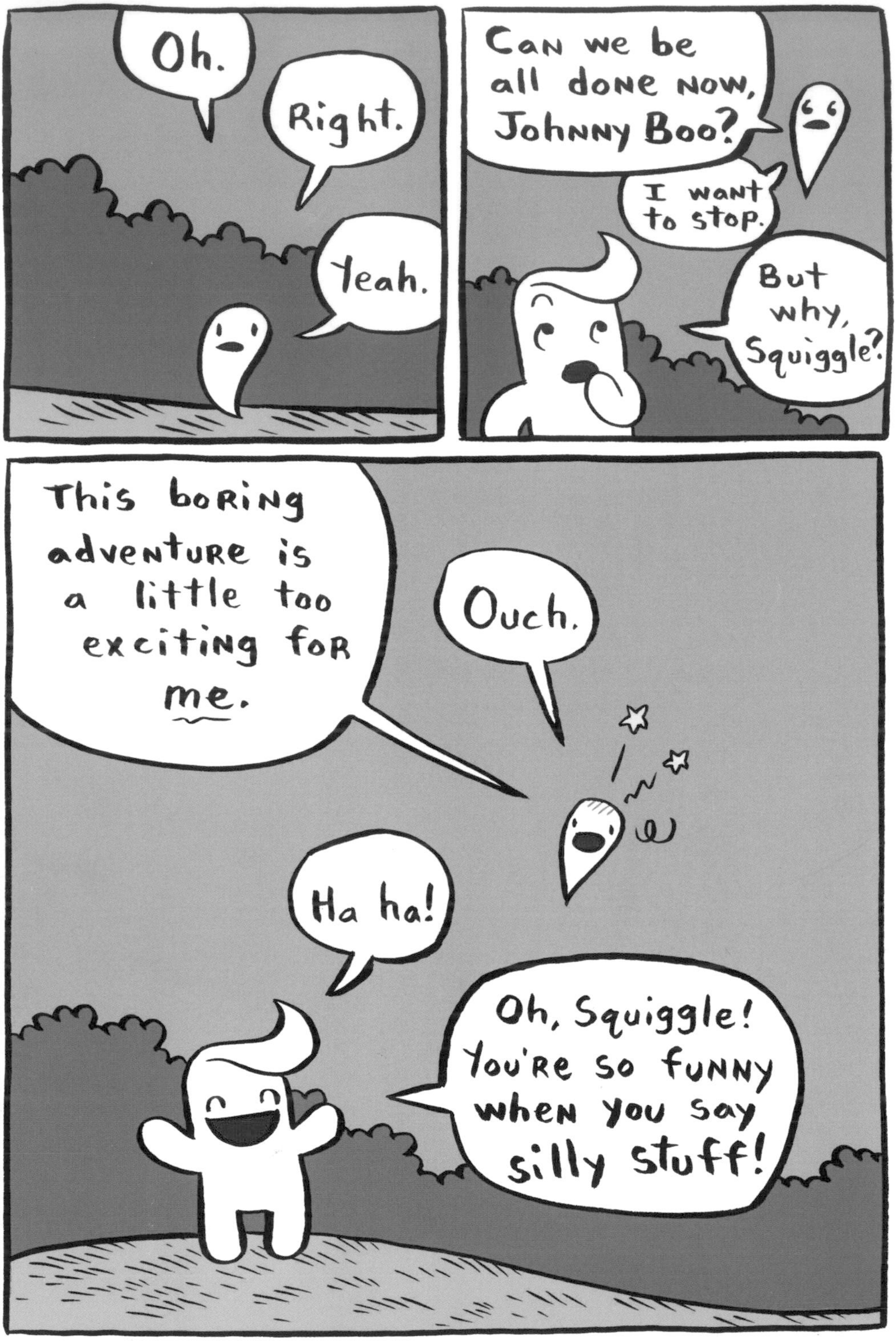
Oh.
Right.
Yeah.
Can we be all done now, Johnny Boo?
I want to stop.
But why, Squiggle?
This boring adventure is a little too exciting for me.
Ouch.
Ha ha!
Oh, Squiggle! You're so funny when you say silly stuff!

CHAPTER TWO:

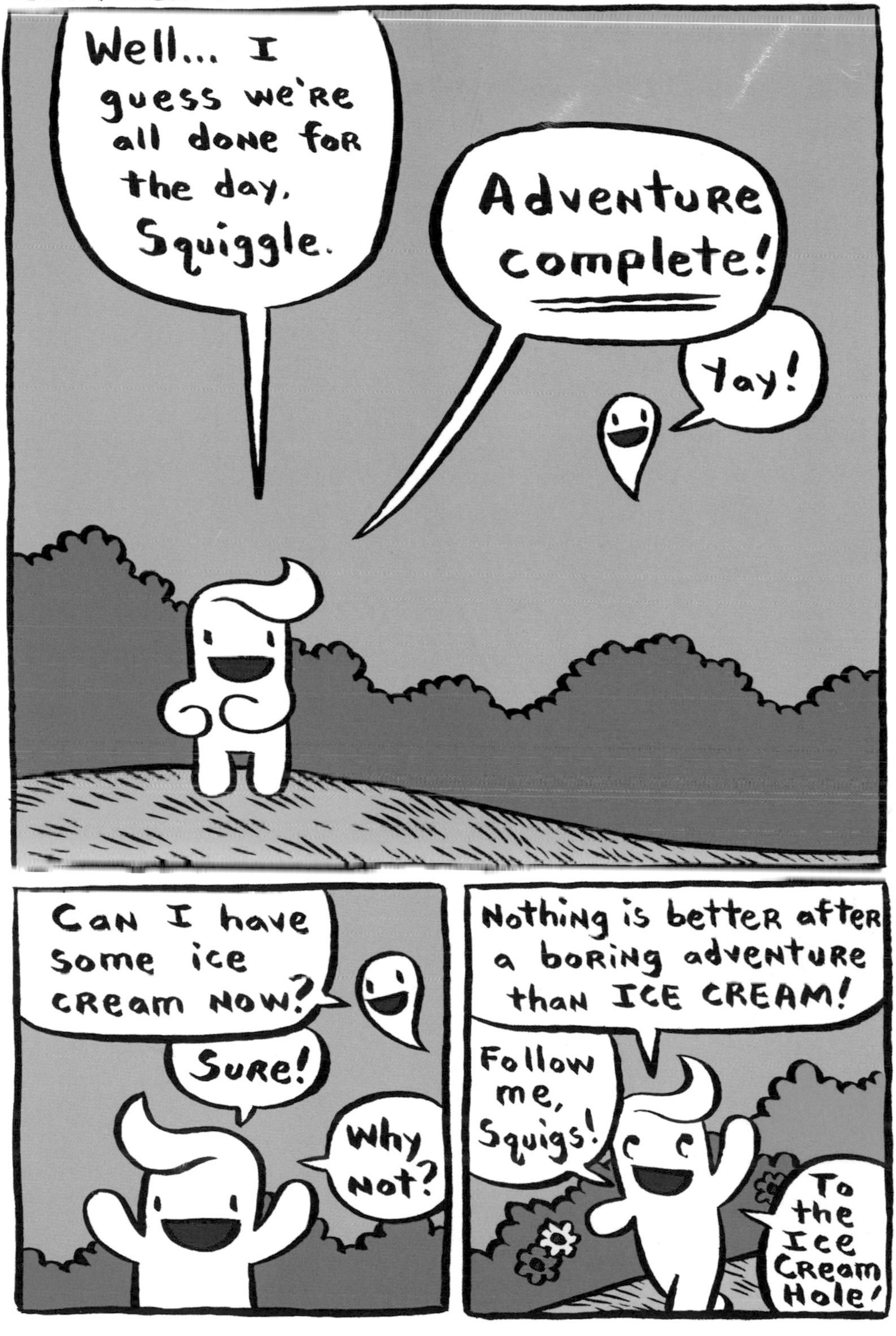
Well... I guess we're all done for the day, Squiggle.
Adventure complete!
Yay!
Can I have some ice cream now?
Sure!
Why not?
Nothing is better after a boring adventure than ICE CREAM!
Follow me, Squigs!
To the Ice Cream Hole!

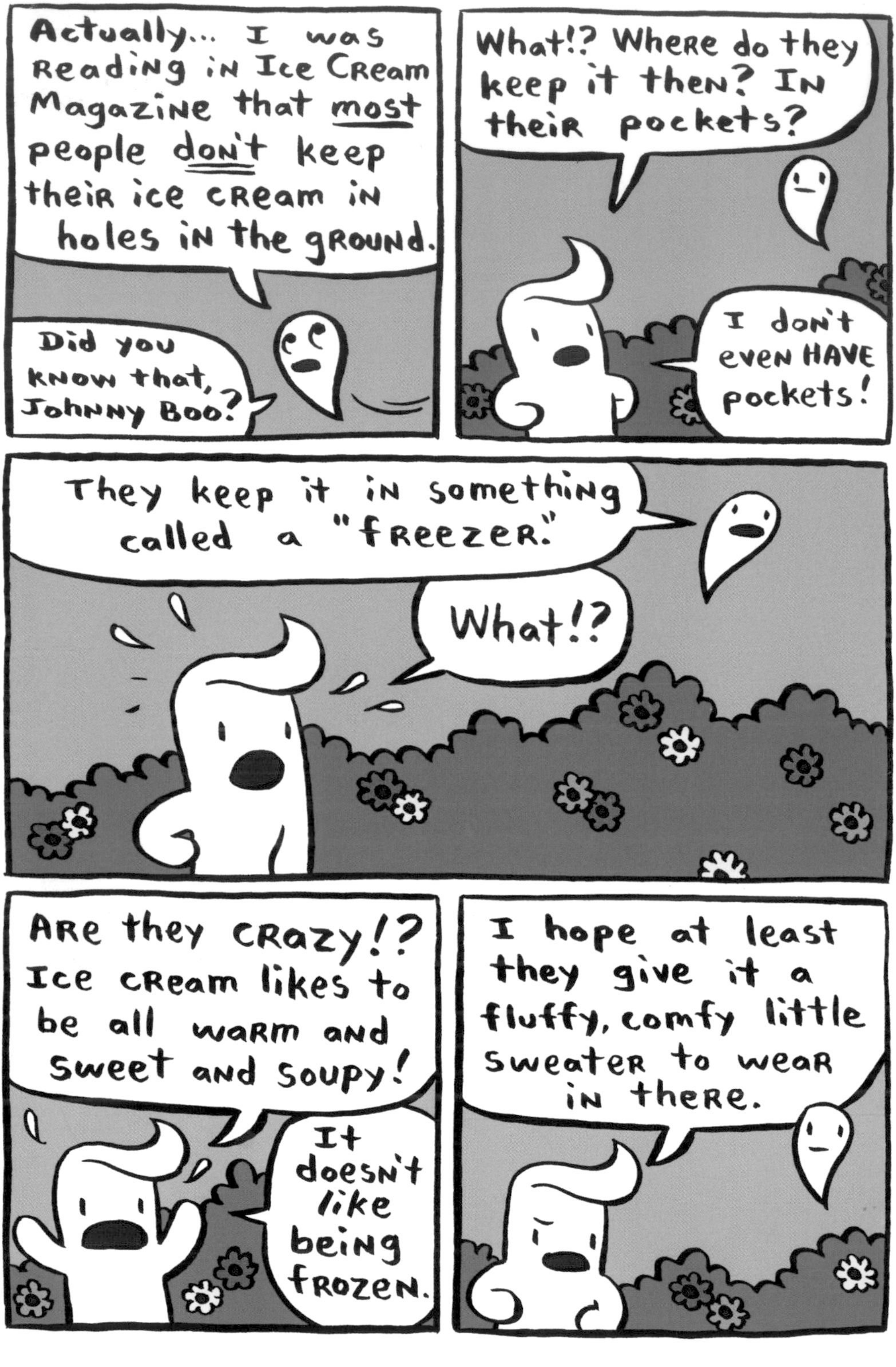

Actually... I was reading in Ice Cream Magazine that most people don't keep their ice cream in holes in the ground.
Did you know that, Johnny Boo?
What!? Where do they keep it then? In their pockets?
I don't even HAVE pockets!
They keep it in something called a "freezer."
What!?
Are they crazy!? Ice cream likes to be all warm and sweet and soupy!
It doesn't like being frozen.
I hope at least they give it a fluffy, comfy little sweater to wear in there.

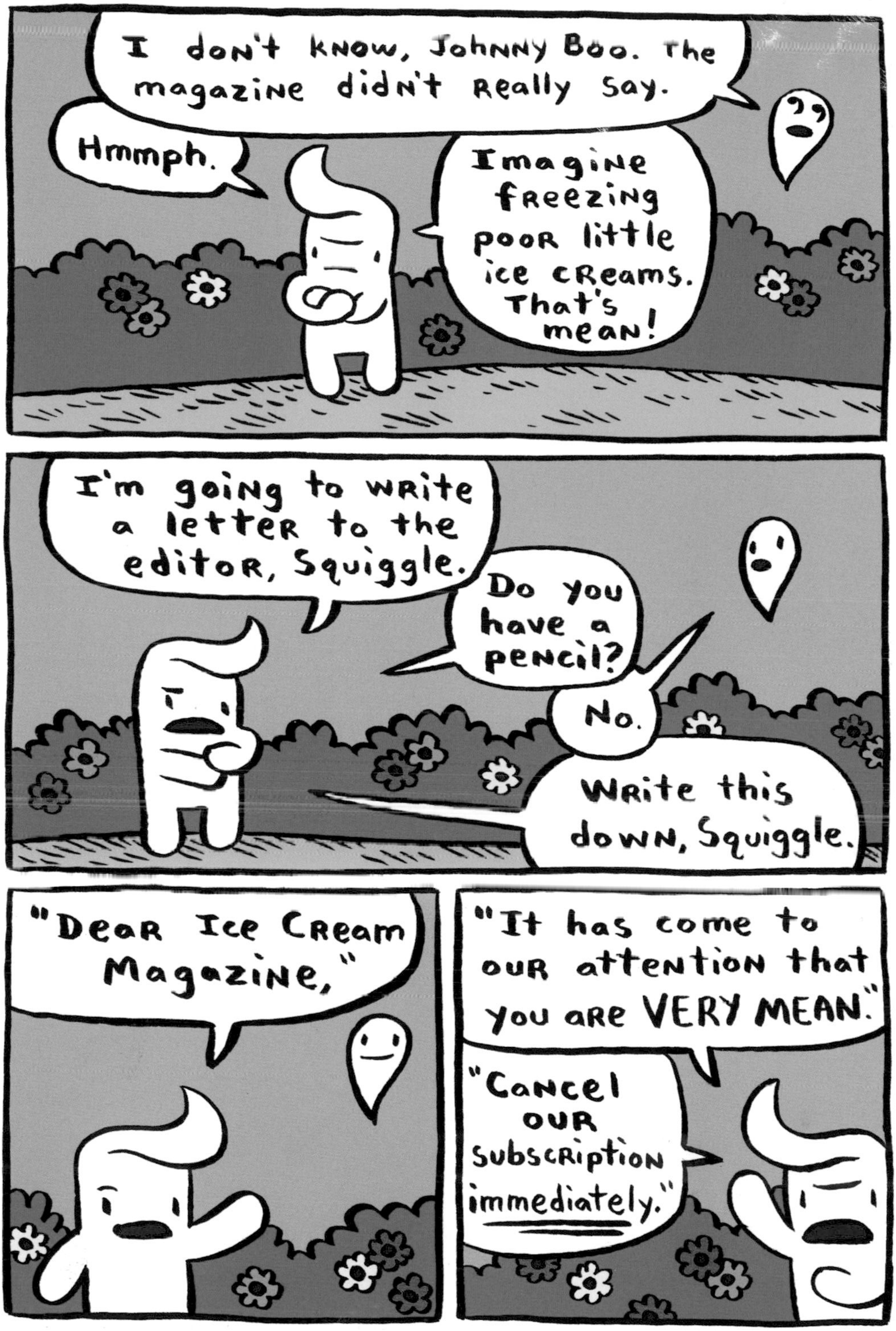
I don't know, Johnny Boo. The magazine didn't really say.
Hmmph.
Imagine freezing poor little ice creams. That's mean!
I'm going to write a letter to the editor, Squiggle.
Do you have a pencil?
No.
Write this down, Squiggle.
"Dear Ice Cream Magazine,"
"It has come to our attention that you are VERY MEAN."
"Cancel our subscription immediately."

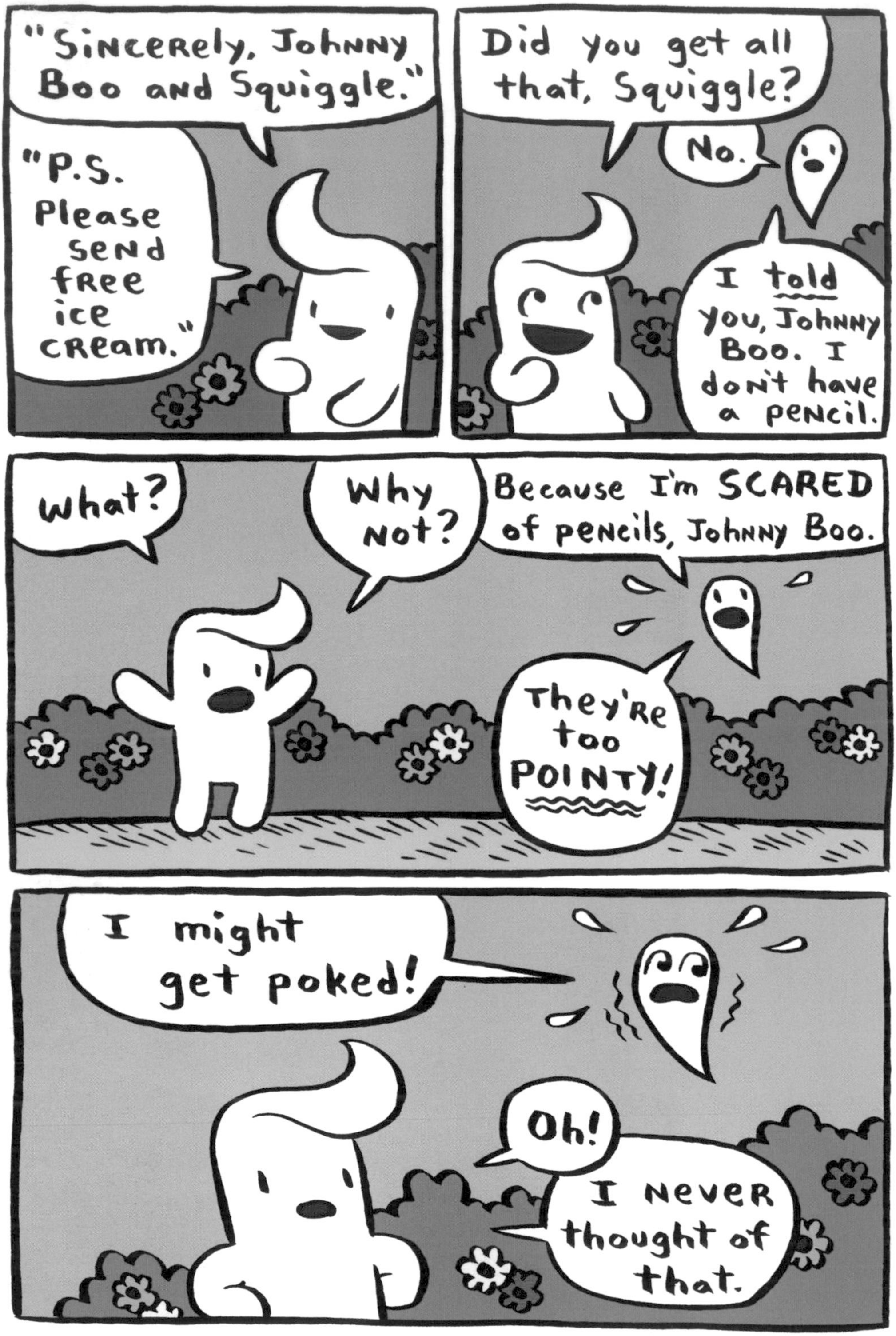
"Sincerely, Johnny Boo and Squiggle."
"P.S. Please send free ice cream."
Did you get all that, Squiggle?
No.
I told you, Johnny Boo. I don't have a pencil.
What?
Why not?
Because I'm SCARED of pencils, Johnny Boo.
They're too POINTY!
I might get poked!
Oh!
I never thought of that.

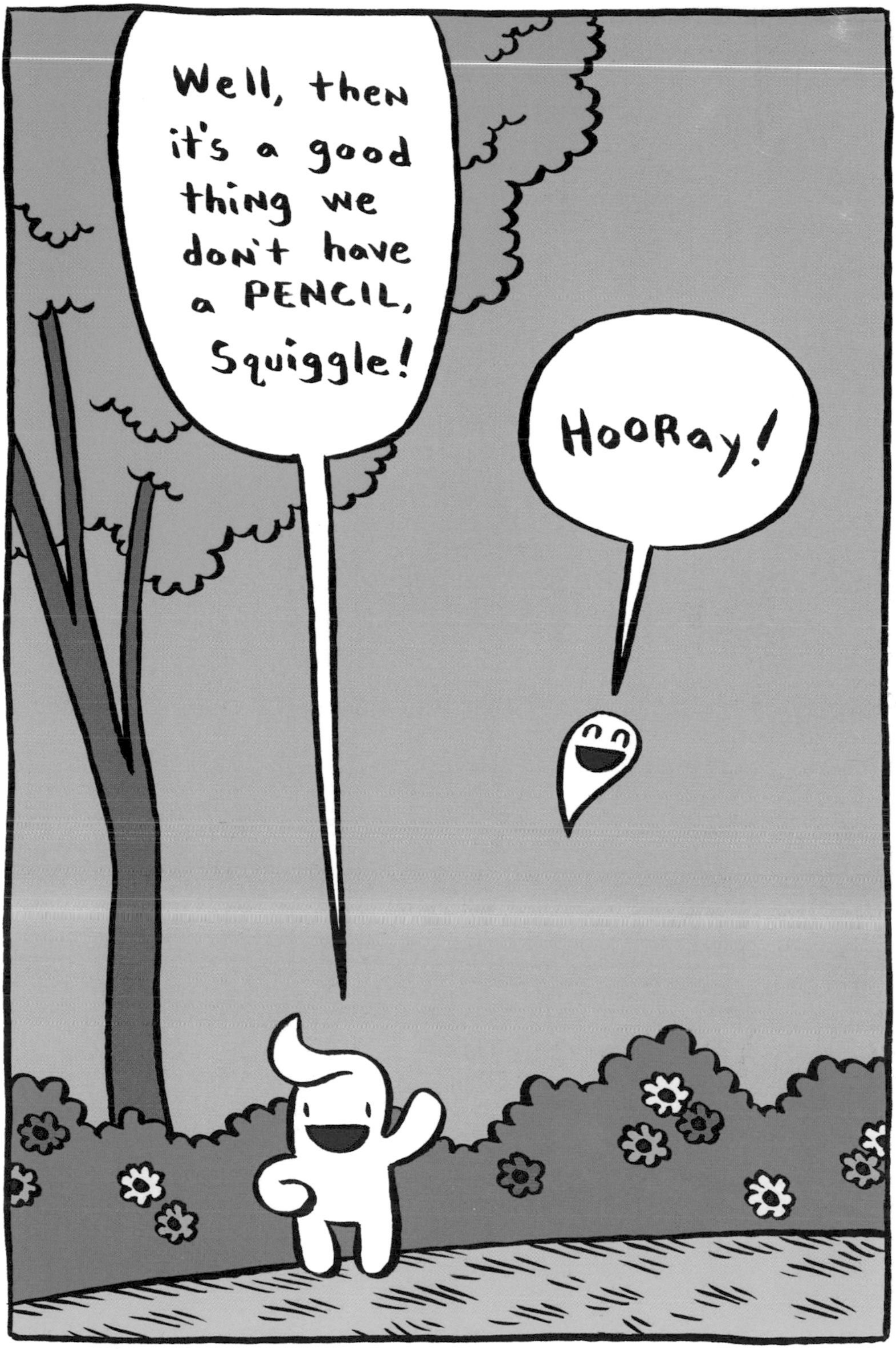
Well, then it's a good thing we don't have a PENCIL, Squiggle!
HooRay!

CHAPTER THREE:

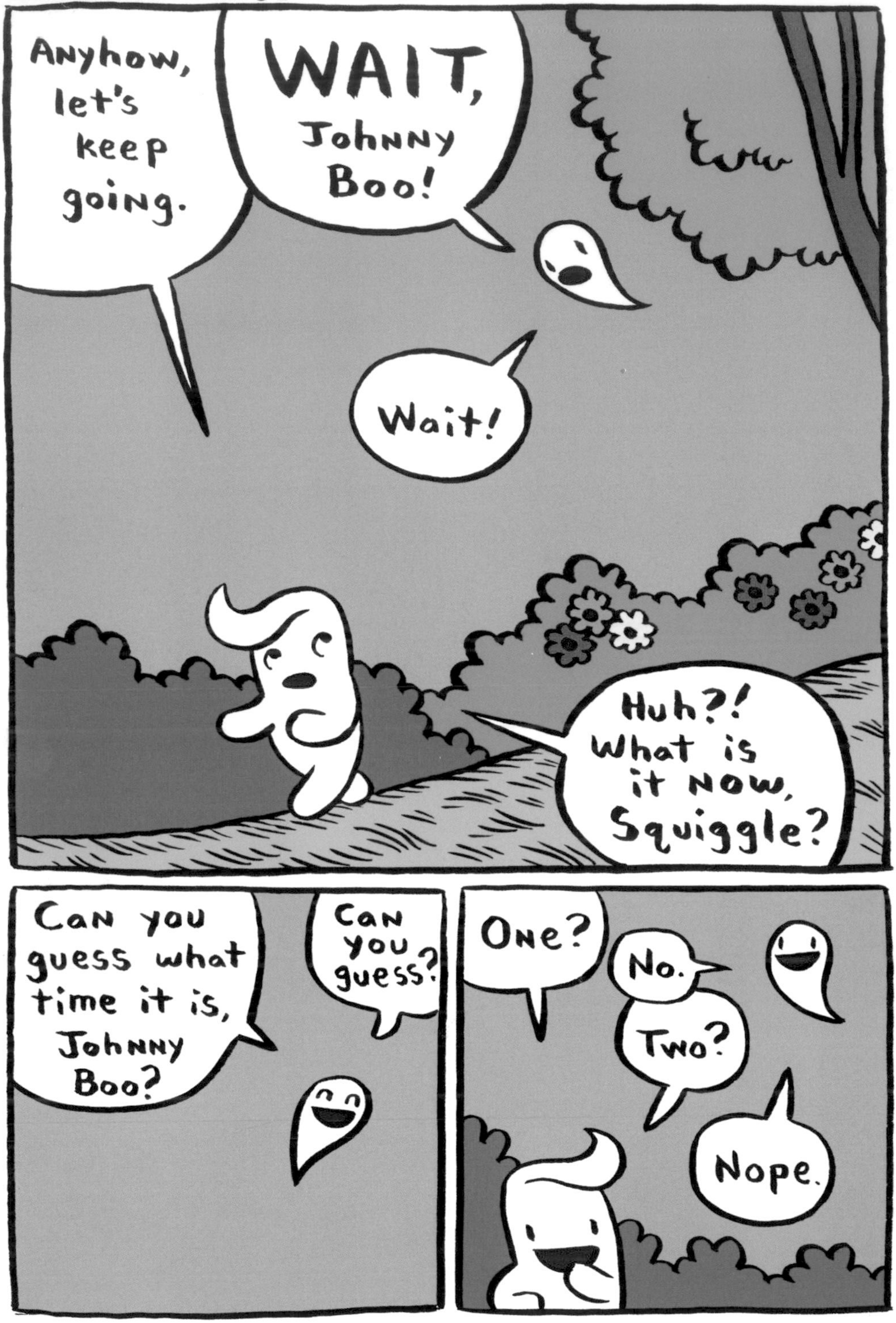
Anyhow, let's keep going.
WAIT, Johnny Boo!
Wait!
Huh?! What is it now, Squiggle?
Can you guess what time it is, Johnny Boo?
Can you guess?
One?
No.
Two?
Nope.

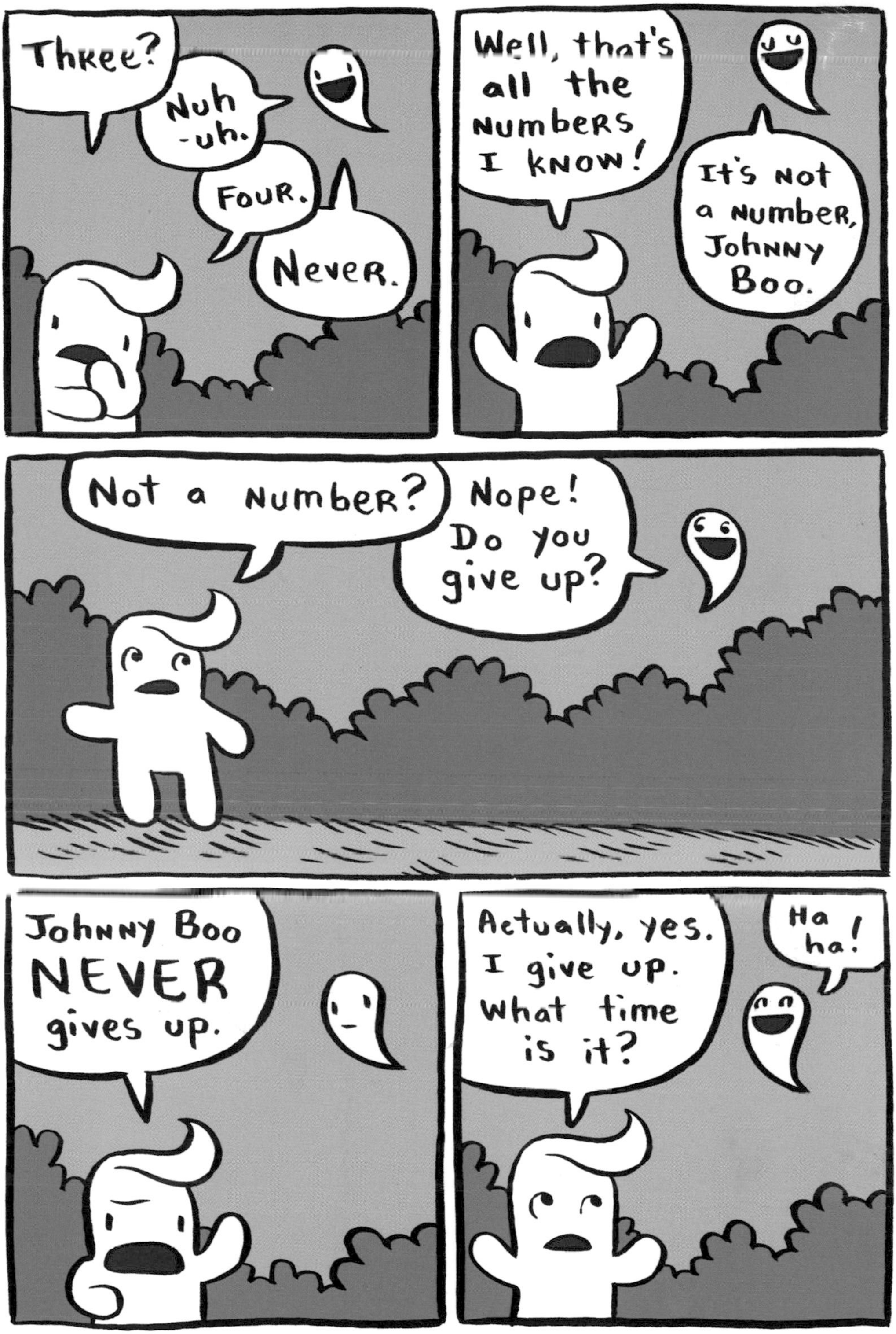
Three?
Nuh -uh.
Four.
Never.
Well, that's all the numbers I know!
It's not a number, Johnny Boo.
Not a number?
Nope! Do you give up?
Johnny Boo NEVER gives up.
Actually, yes. I give up. What time is it?
Ha ha!

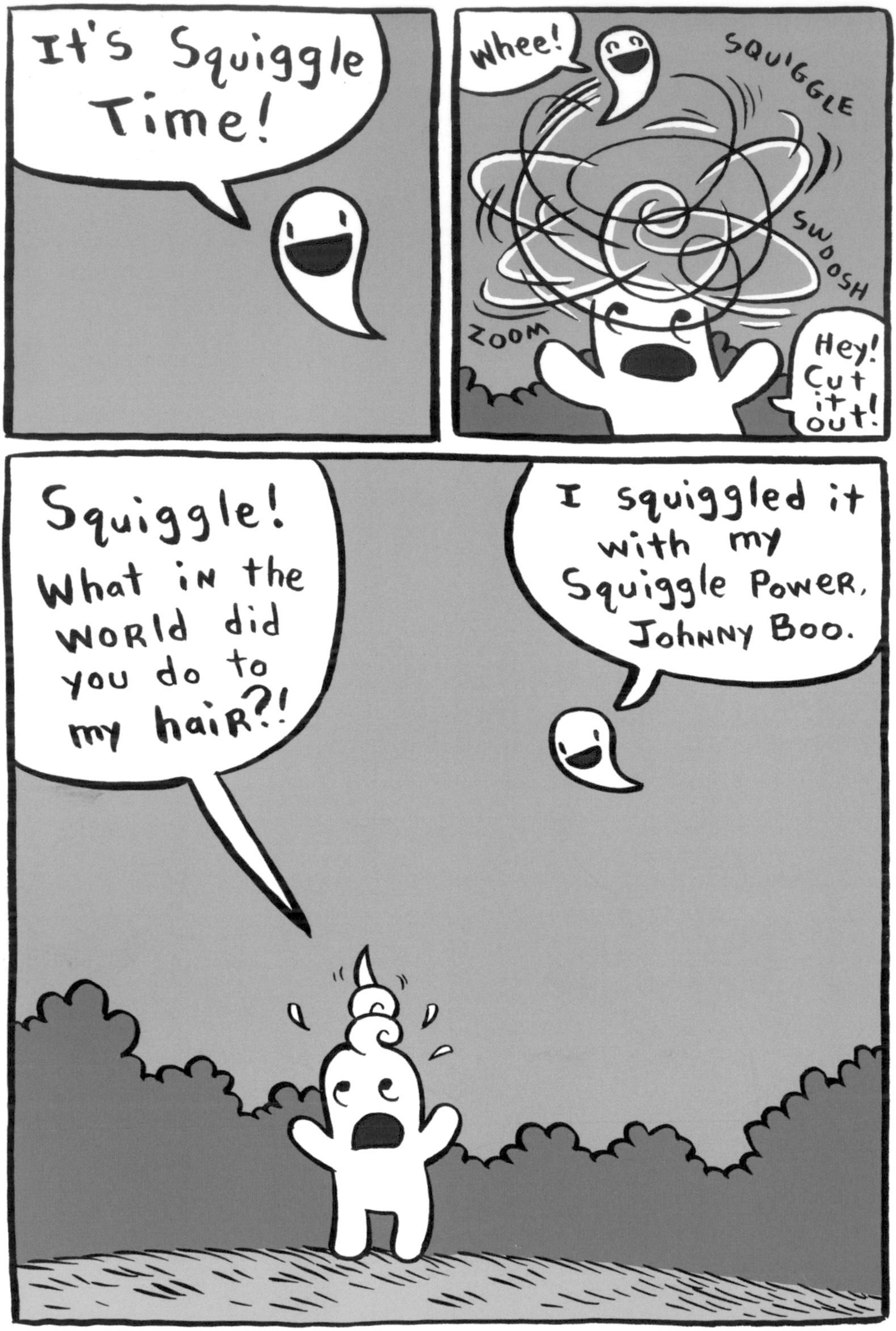
It's Squiggle Time!
Whee!
SQUIGGLE
SWOOSH
ZOOM
Hey! Cut it out!
Squiggle! What in the WORLD did you do to my hair?!
I squiggled it with my Squiggle Power, Johnny Boo.

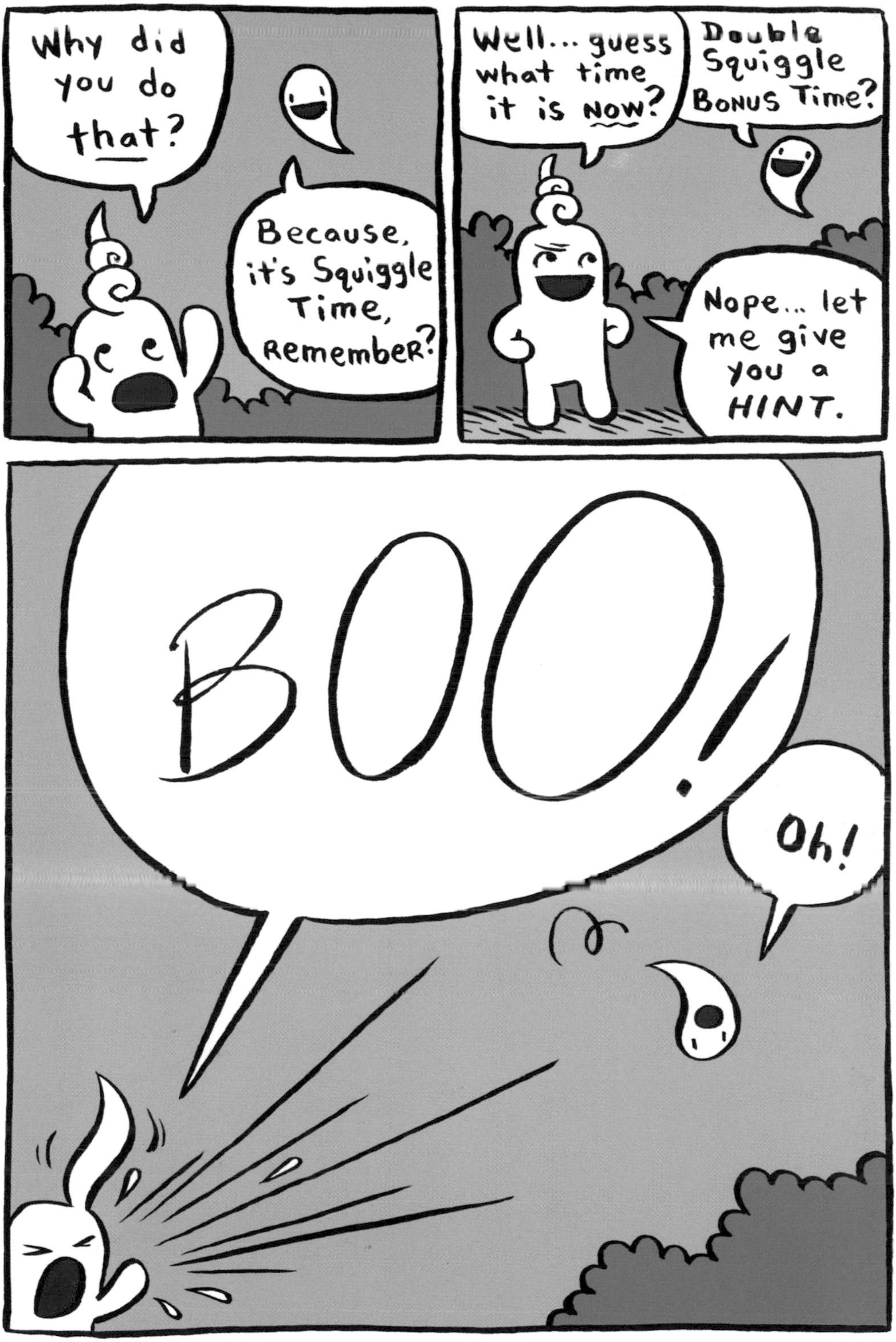
Why did you do that?
Because, it's Squiggle Time, remember?
Well... guess what time it is NOW?
Double Squiggle Bonus Time?
Nope... let me give you a HINT.
BOO!
Oh!

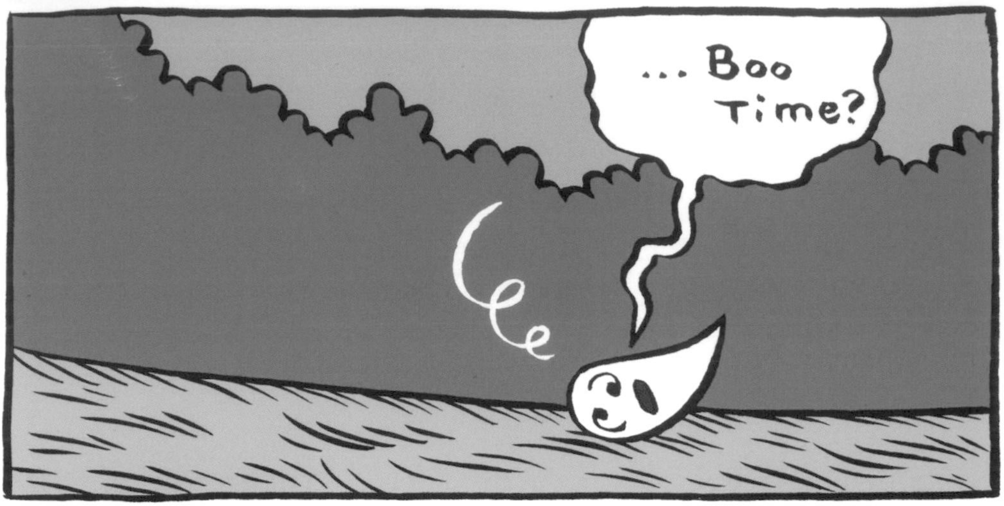
... Boo Time?

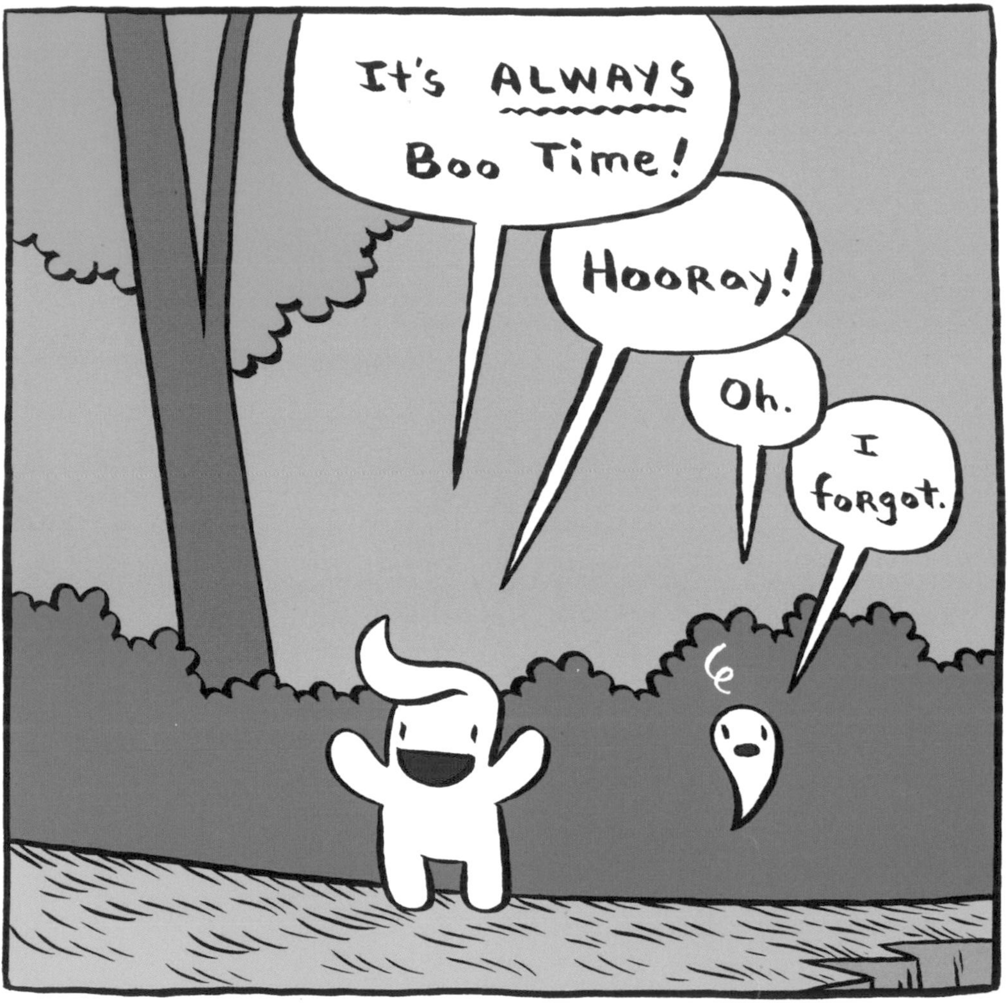
It's ALWAYS Boo Time!
Hooray!
Oh.
I forgot.

CHAPTER FOUR:

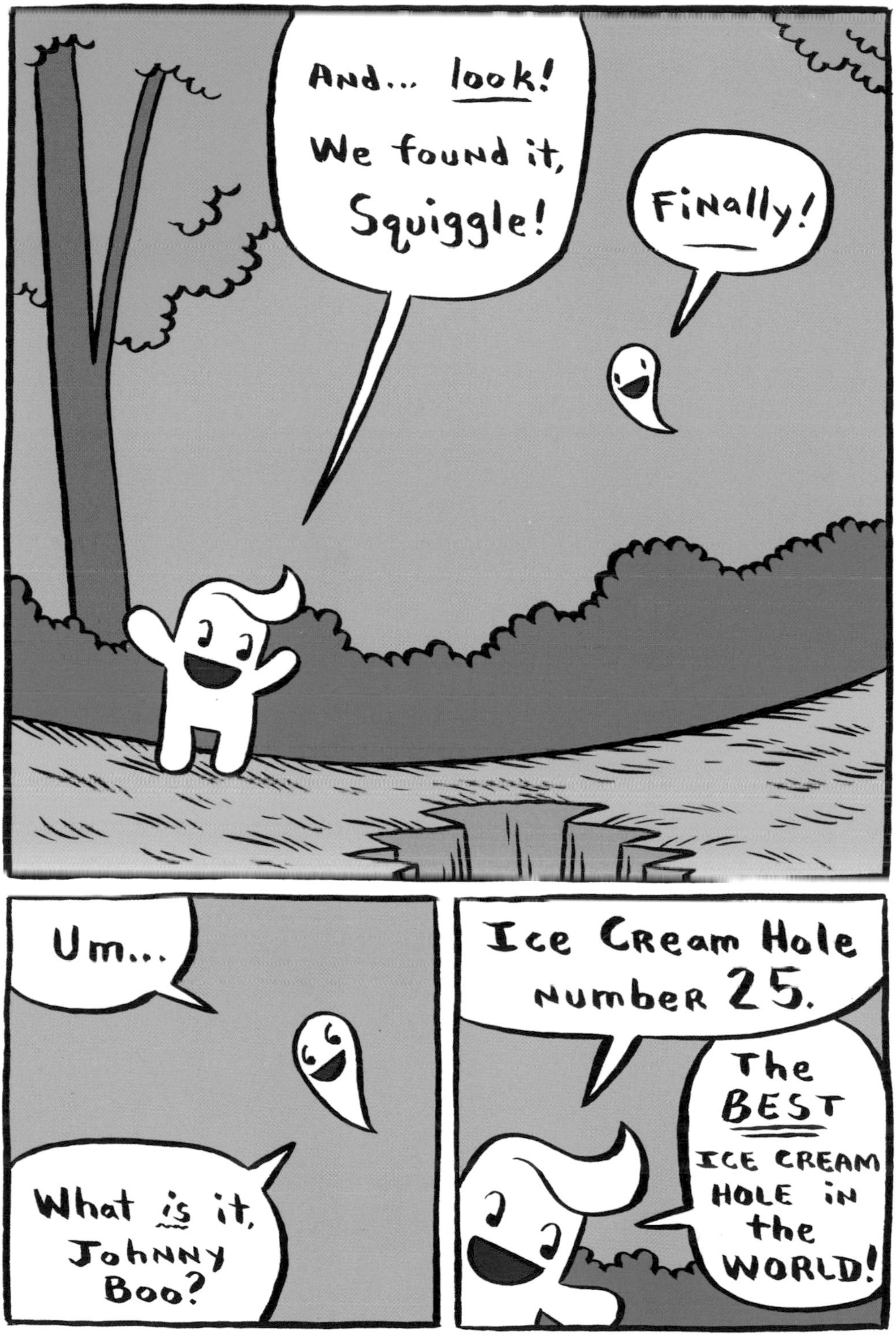
And... look! We found it, Squiggle!
Finally!
Um...
What is it, Johnny Boo?
Ice Cream Hole number 25.
The BEST ICE CREAM HOLE in the WORLD!

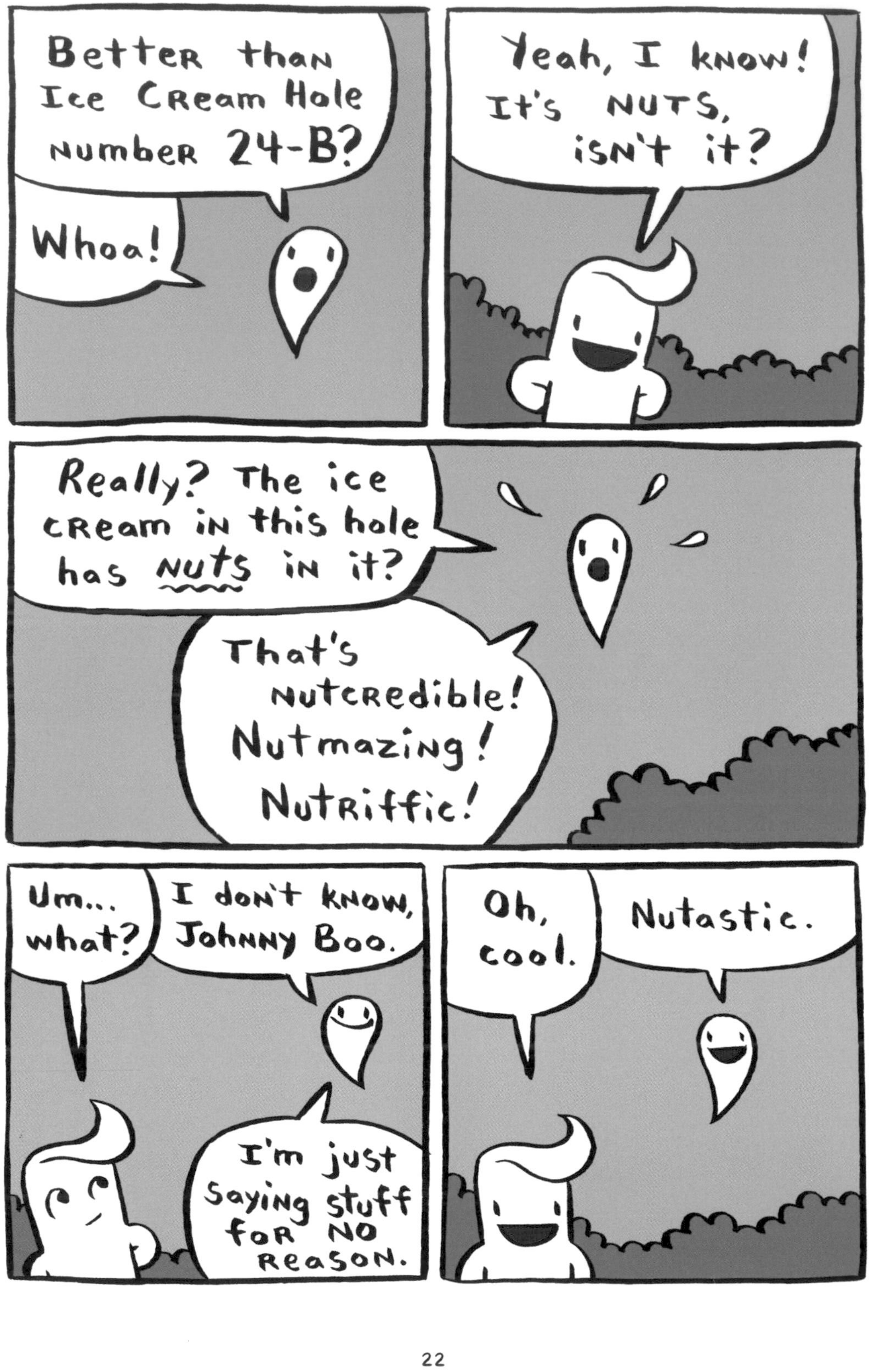
Better than Ice Cream Hole number 24-B?
Whoa!
Yeah, I know! It's NUTS, isn't it?
Really? The ice cream in this hole has NUTS in it?
That's Nutcredible! Nutmazing! Nutriffic!
Um... what?
I don't know, Johnny Boo.
I'm just saying stuff for NO reason.
Oh, cool.
Nutastic.

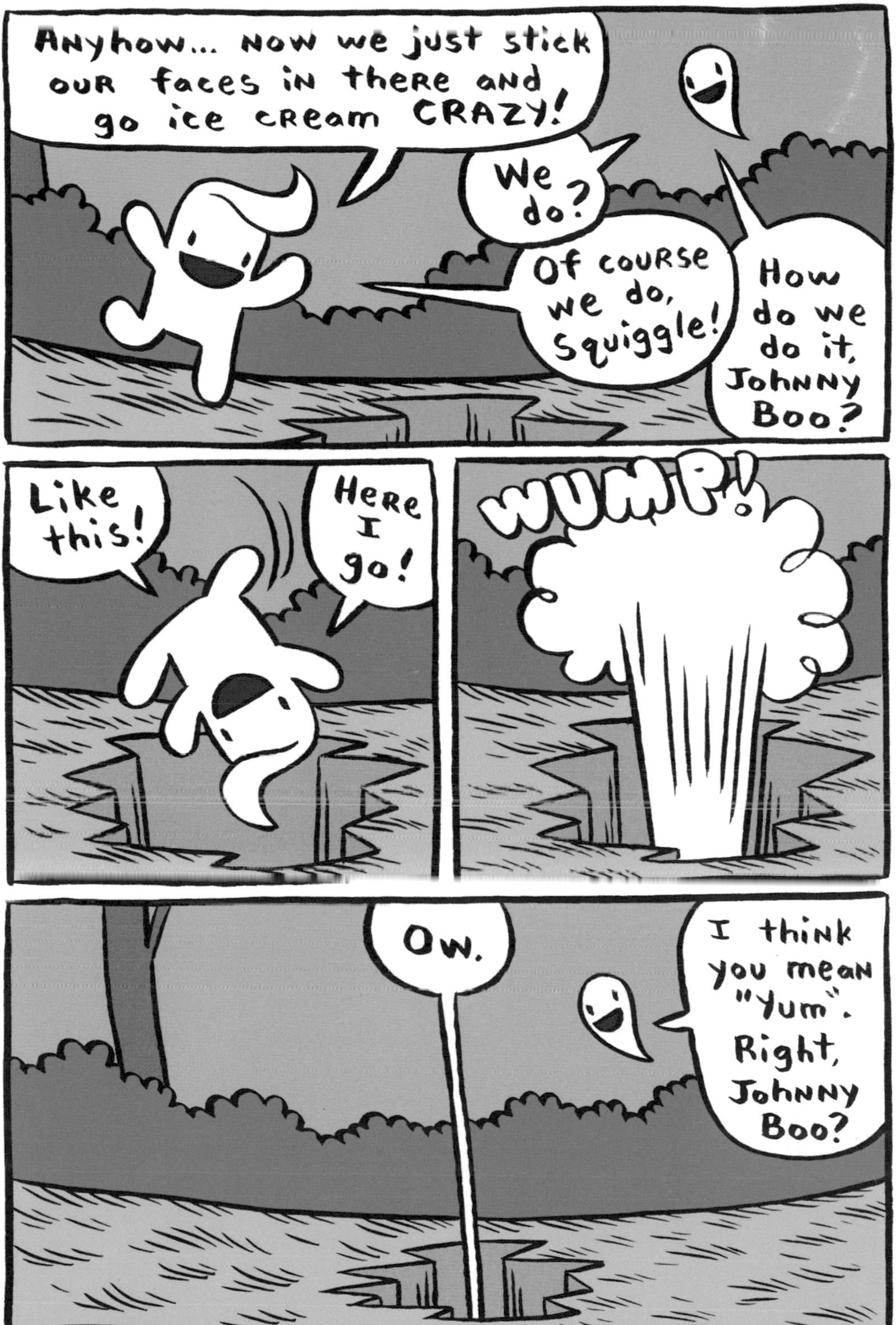
Anyhow... Now we just stick our faces in there and go ice cream CRAZY!
We do?
Of course we do, Squiggle!
How do we do it, Johnny Boo?
Like this!
Here I go!
WUMP!
Ow.
I think you mean "Yum". Right, Johnny Boo?

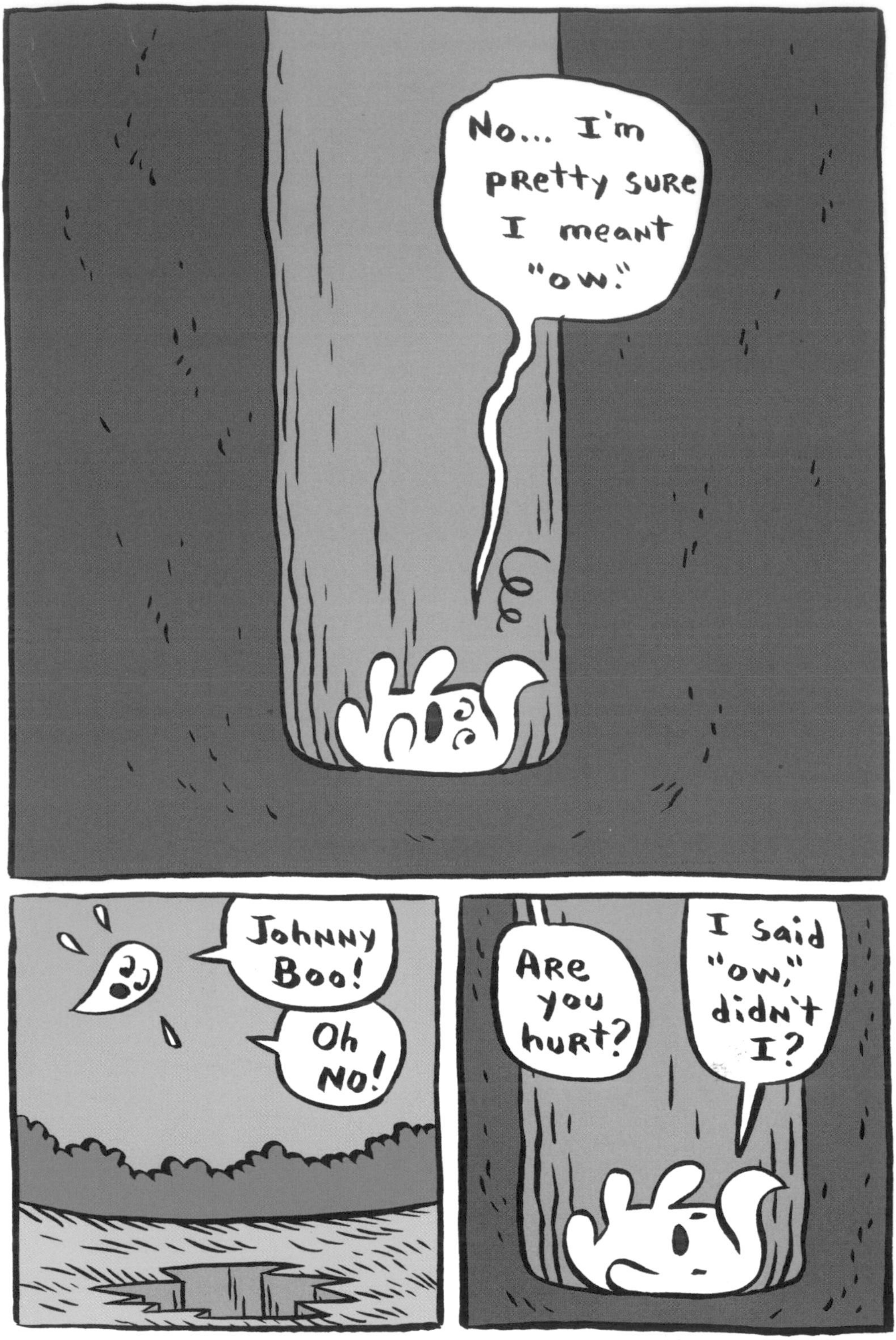
No... I'm pretty sure I meant "ow."
Johnny Boo!
Oh No!
Are you hurt?
I said "ow," didn't I?

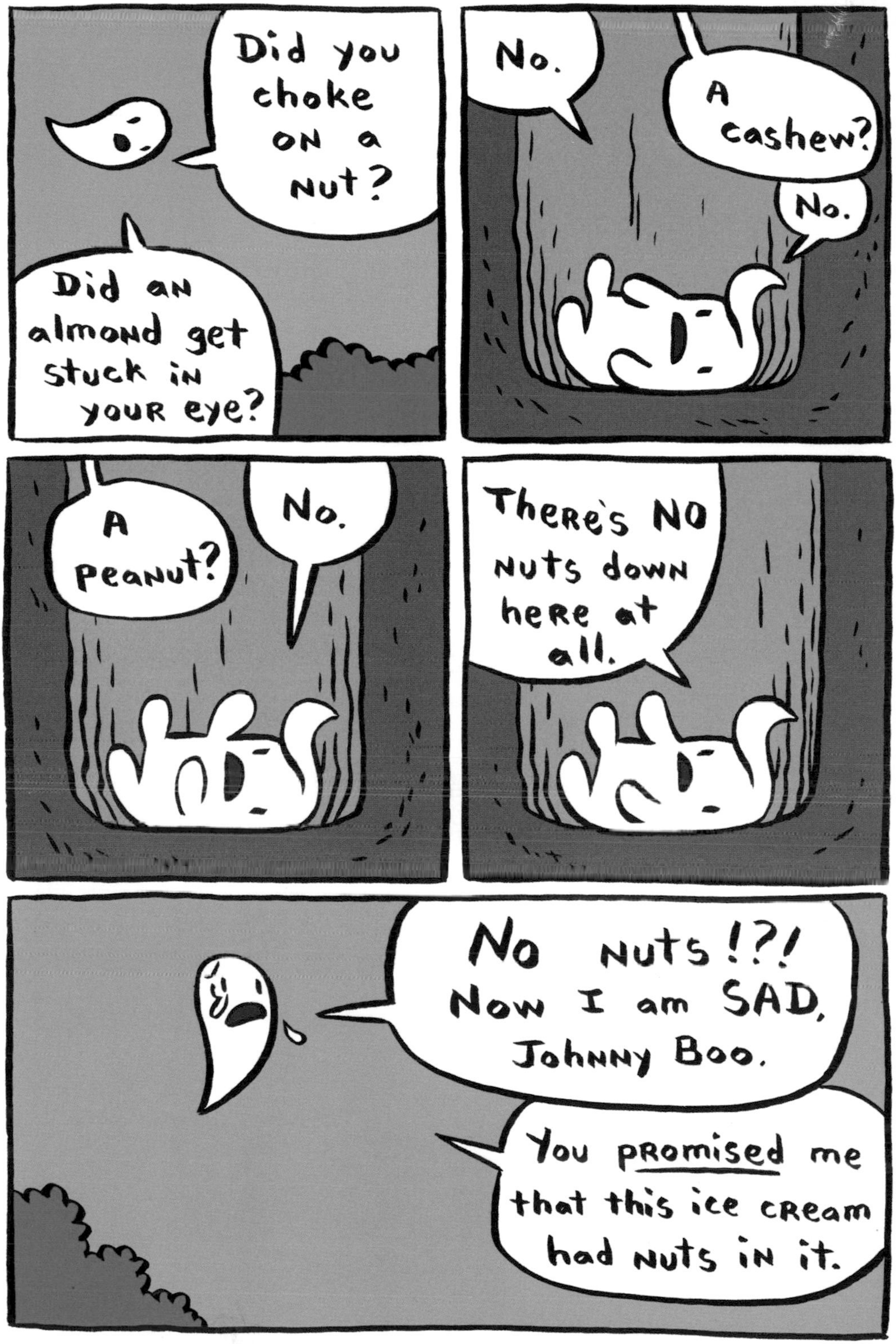
Did you choke on a nut?
Did an almond get stuck in your eye?
No.
A cashew?
No.
A peanut?
No.
There's NO nuts down here at all.
No nuts!?! Now I am SAD, Johnny Boo.
You promised me that this ice cream had nuts in it.

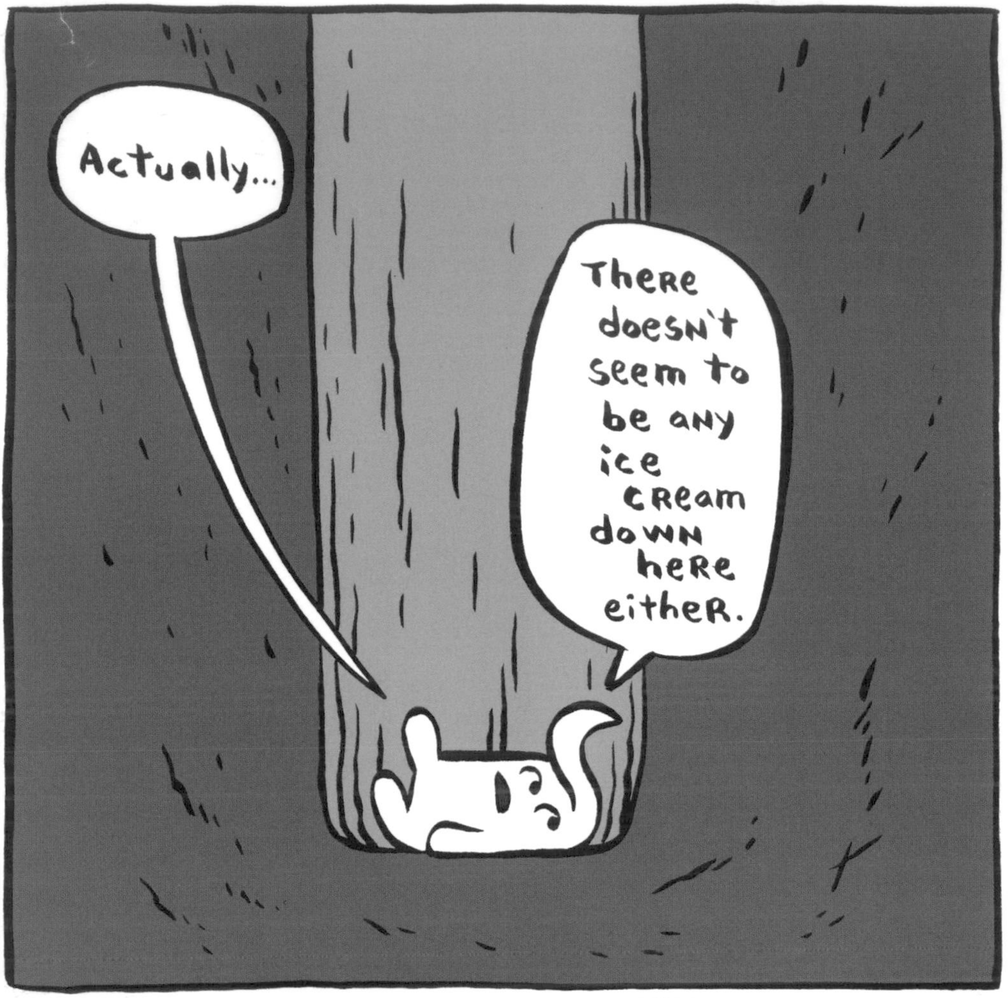
Actually...
There doesn't seem to be any ice cream down here either.

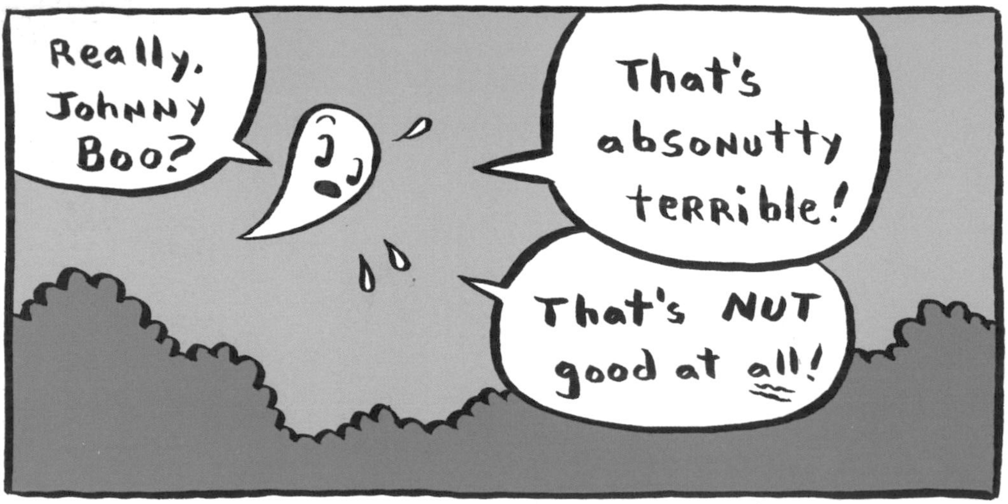
Really. Johnny Boo?
That's absonutty terrible!
That's NUT good at all!

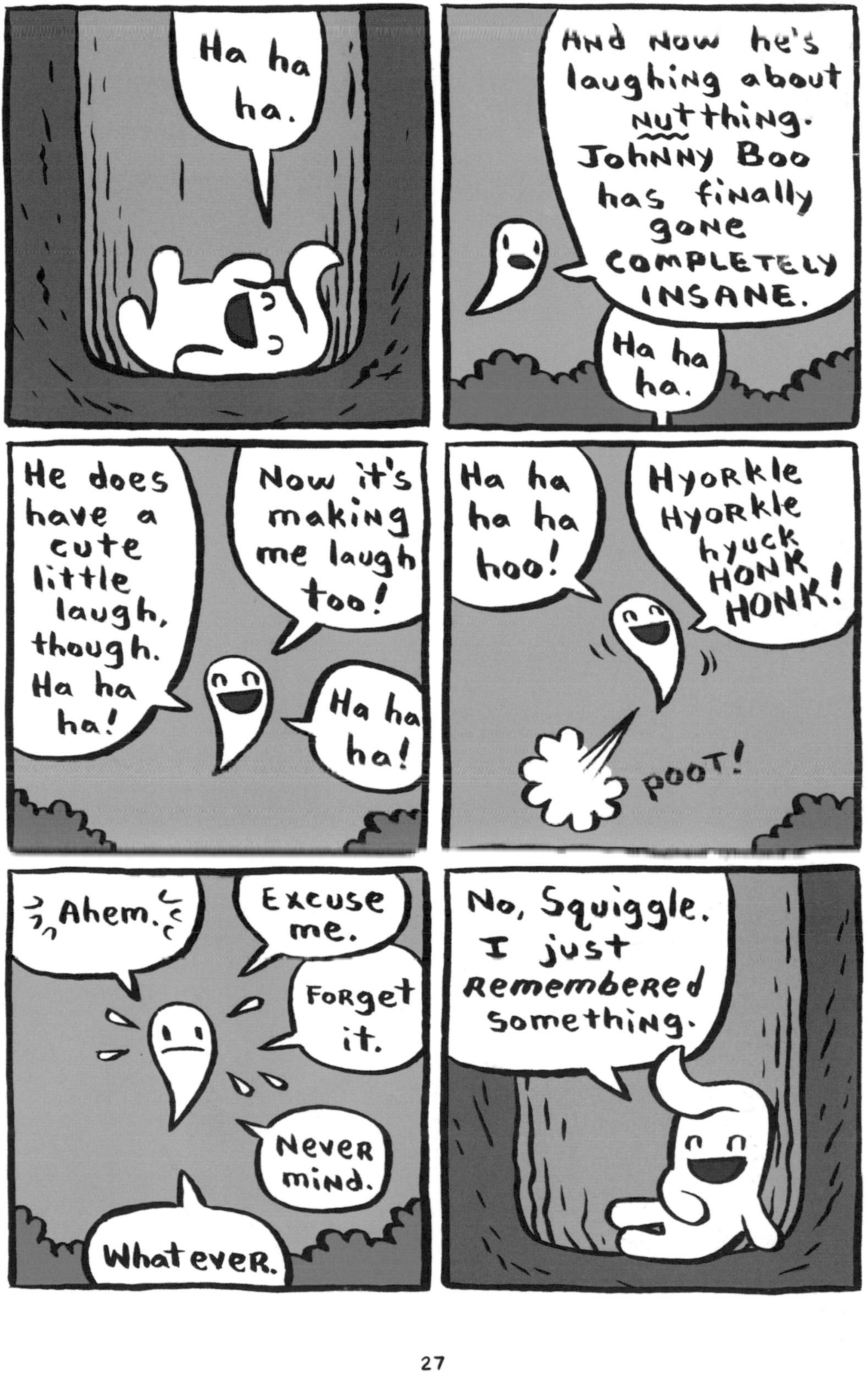
Ha ha ha.
And Now he's laughing about NUTthing. Johnny Boo has finally gone COMPLETELY INSANE.
Ha ha ha.
He does have a cute little laugh, though. Ha ha ha!
Now it's making me laugh too!
Ha ha ha!
Ha ha ha ha hoo!
Hyorkle Hyorkle hyuck HONK HONK!
POOT!
Ahem.
Excuse me.
Forget it.
Never mind.
Whatever.
No, Squiggle. I just remembered something.

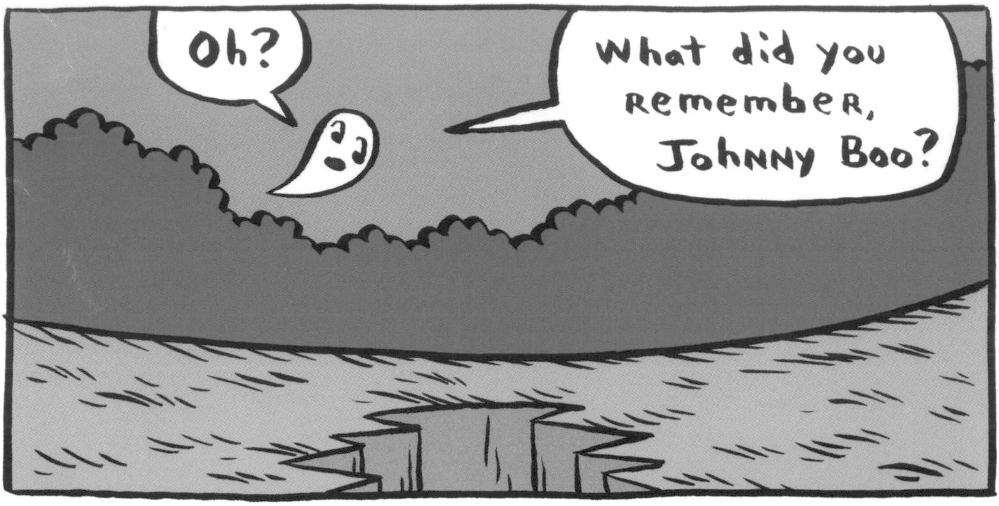
Oh?
What did you remember, Johnny Boo?

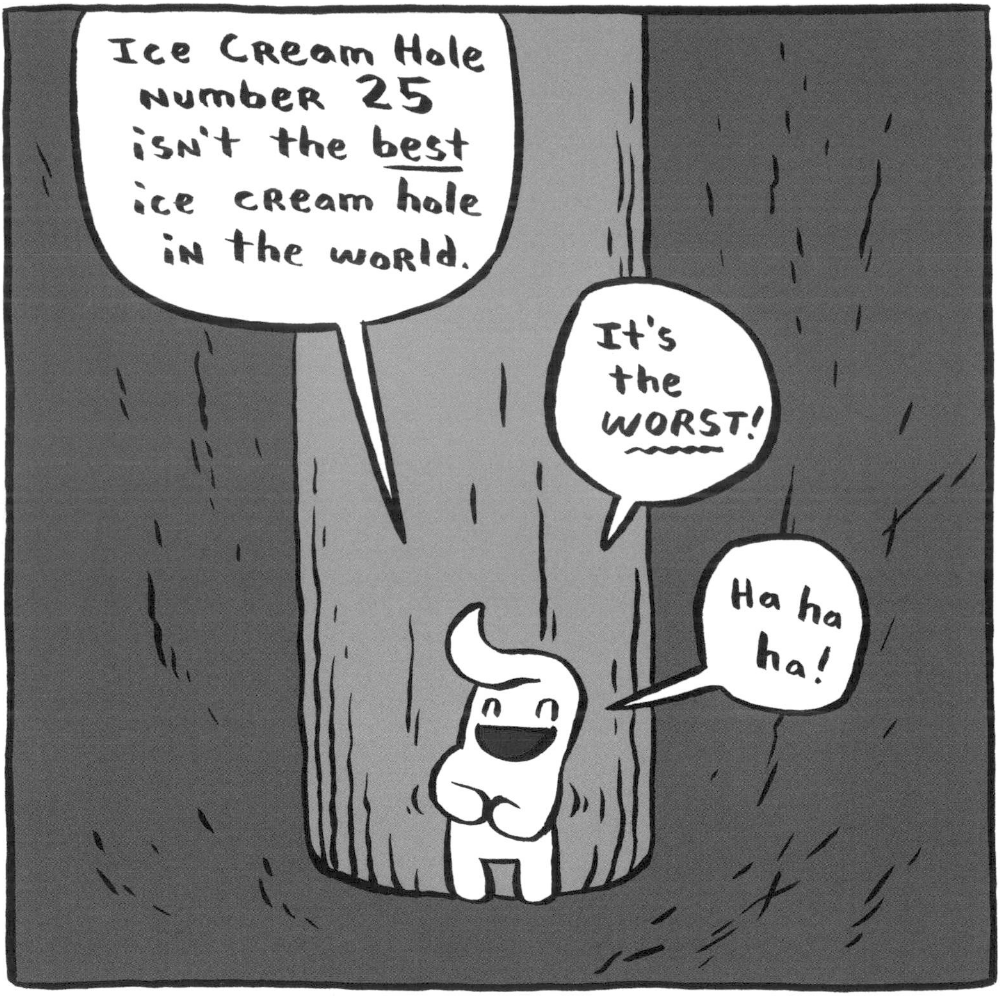
Ice Cream Hole number 25 isn't the best ice cream hole in the world.
It's the WORST!
Ha ha ha!

CHAPTER FIVE:

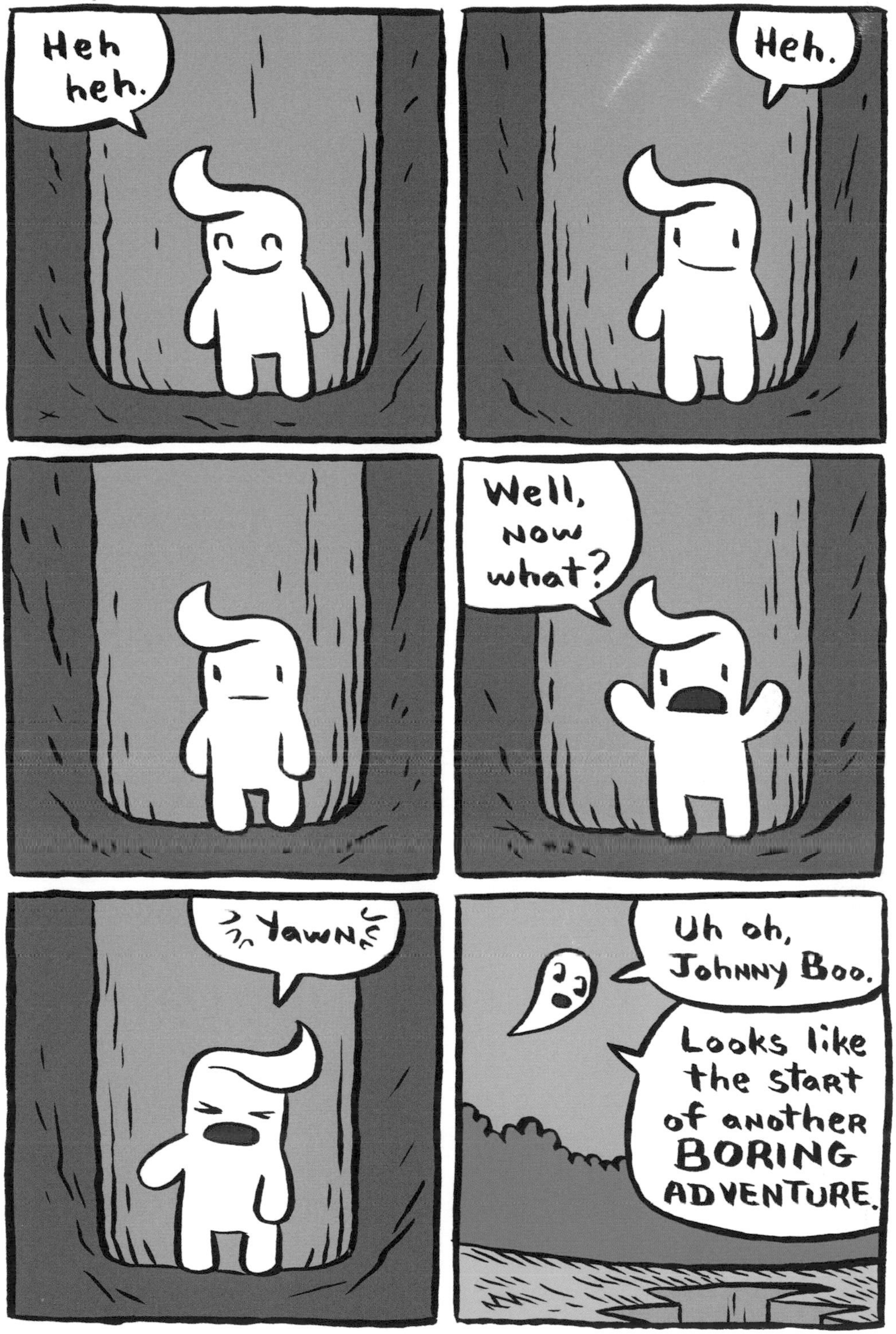
Heh heh.
Heh.
Well, now what?
Yawn
Uh oh, Johnny Boo.
Looks like the start of another BORING ADVENTURE.

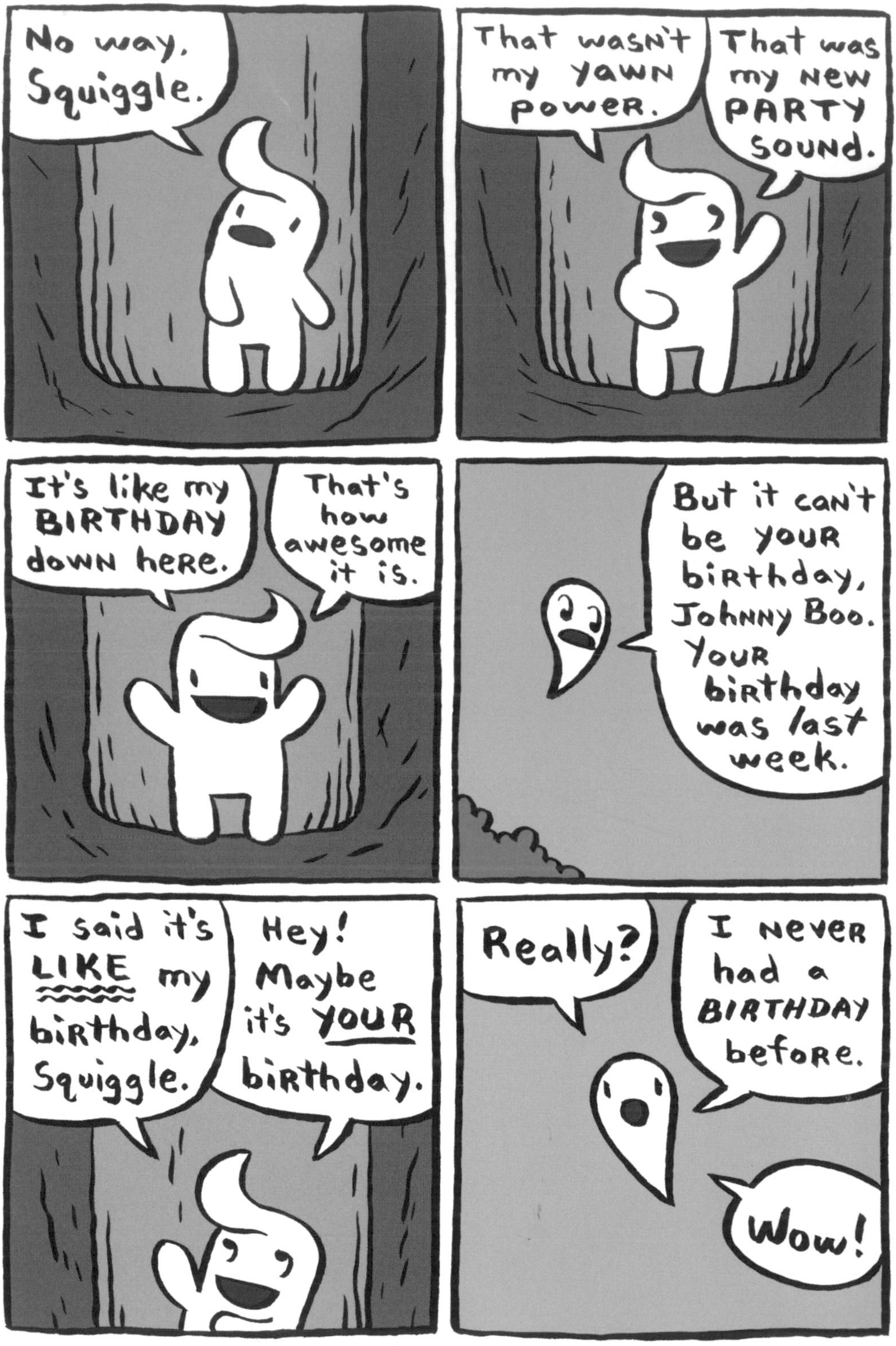
No way, Squiggle.
That wasn't my YAWN POWER.
That was my NEW PARTY SOUND.
It's like my BIRTHDAY down here.
That's how awesome it is.
But it can't be YOUR birthday, Johnny Boo. YOUR birthday was last week.
I said it's LIKE my birthday, Squiggle.
Hey! Maybe it's YOUR birthday.
Really?
I never had a BIRTHDAY before.
Wow!

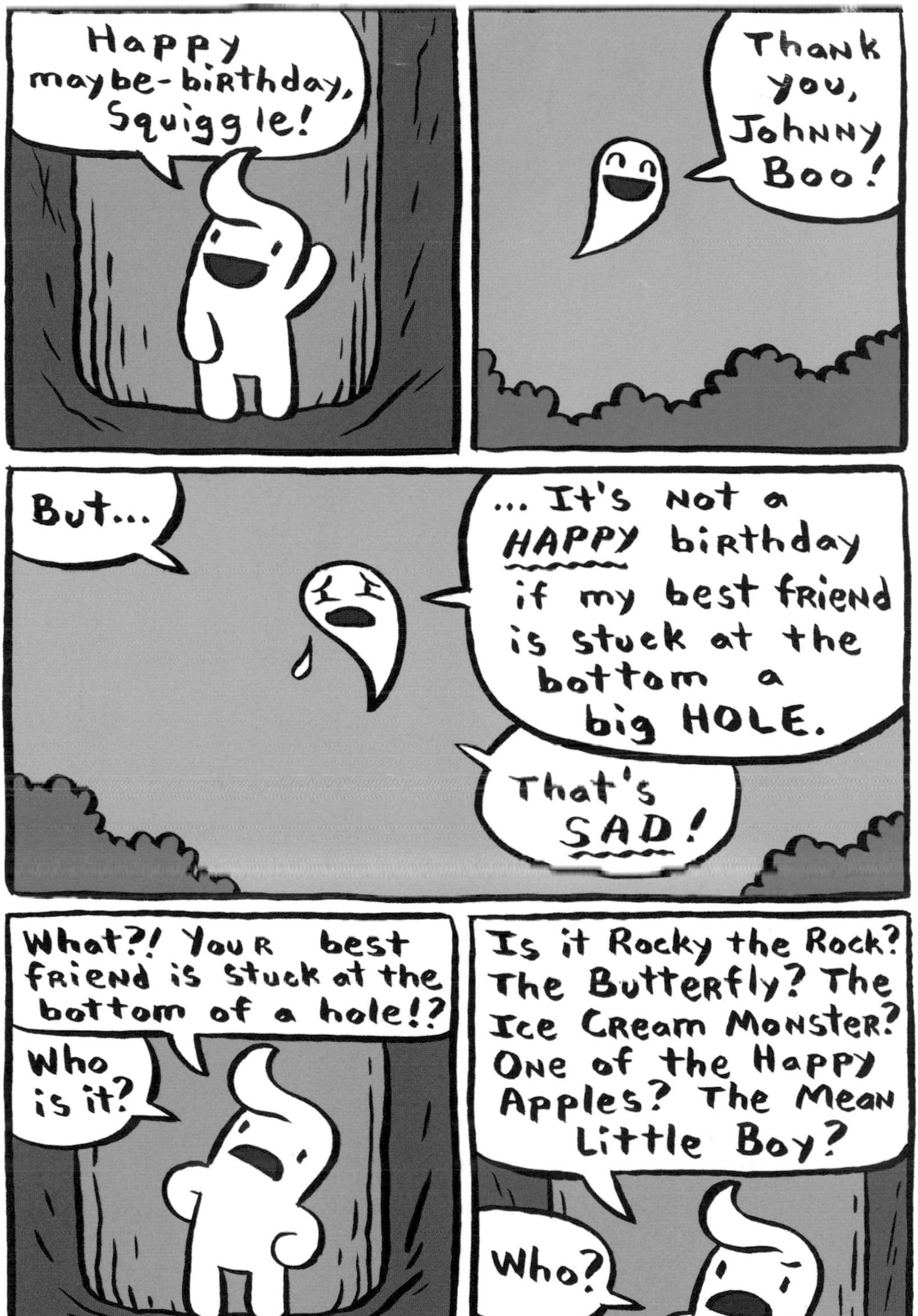
Happy maybe-birthday, Squiggle!
Thank you, Johnny Boo!
But...
...It's not a HAPPY birthday if my best friend is stuck at the bottom a big HOLE.
That's SAD!
What?! Your best friend is stuck at the bottom of a hole!?
Who is it?
Is it Rocky the Rock? The Butterfly? The Ice Cream Monster? One of the Happy Apples? The Mean Little Boy?
Who?

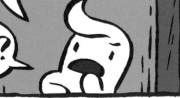

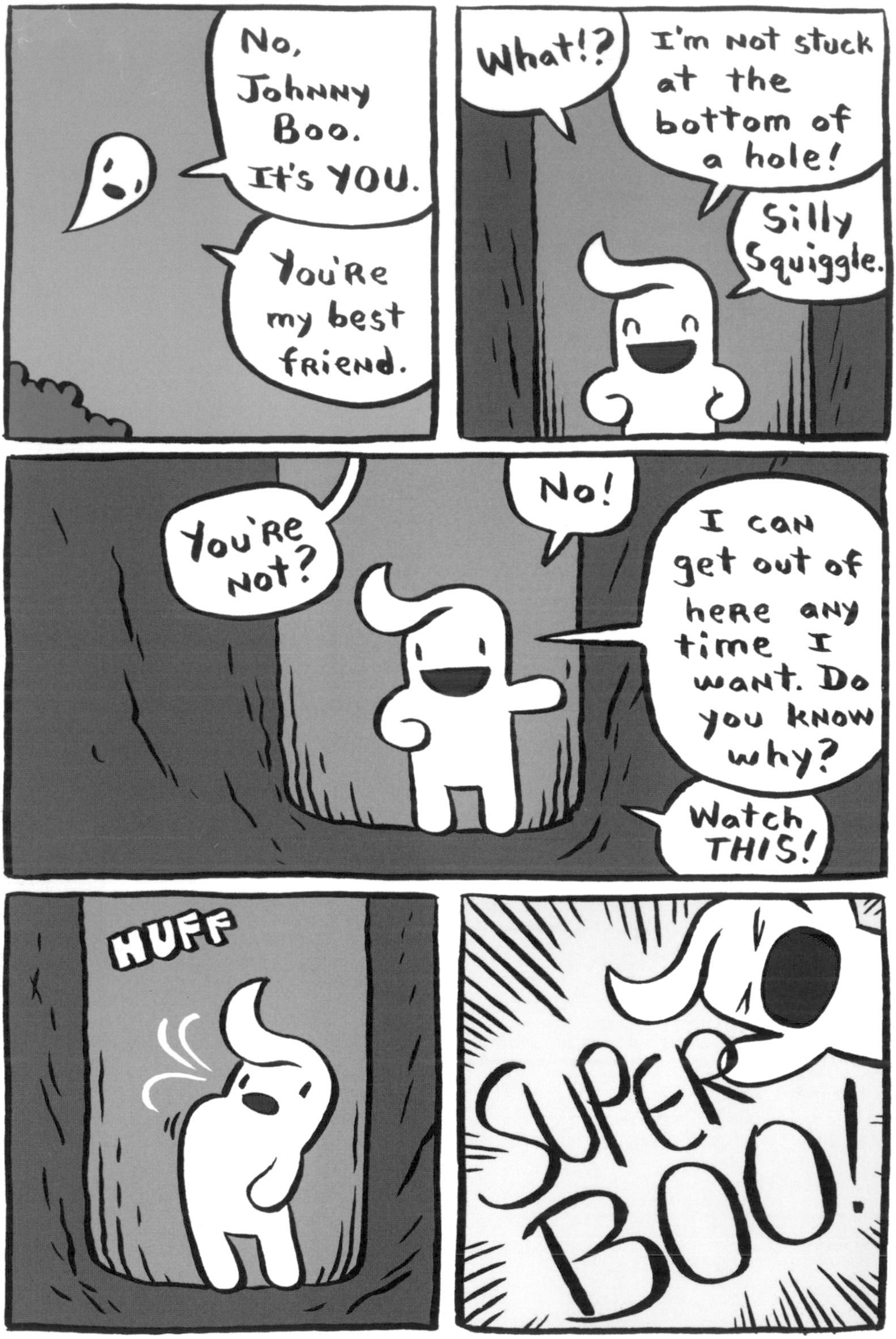
No, Johnny Boo. It's YOU.
You're my best friend.
What!?
I'm not stuck at the bottom of a hole!
Silly Squiggle.
You're not?
No!
I can get out of here any time I want. Do you know why?
Watch THIS!
HUFF
SUPER BOO!

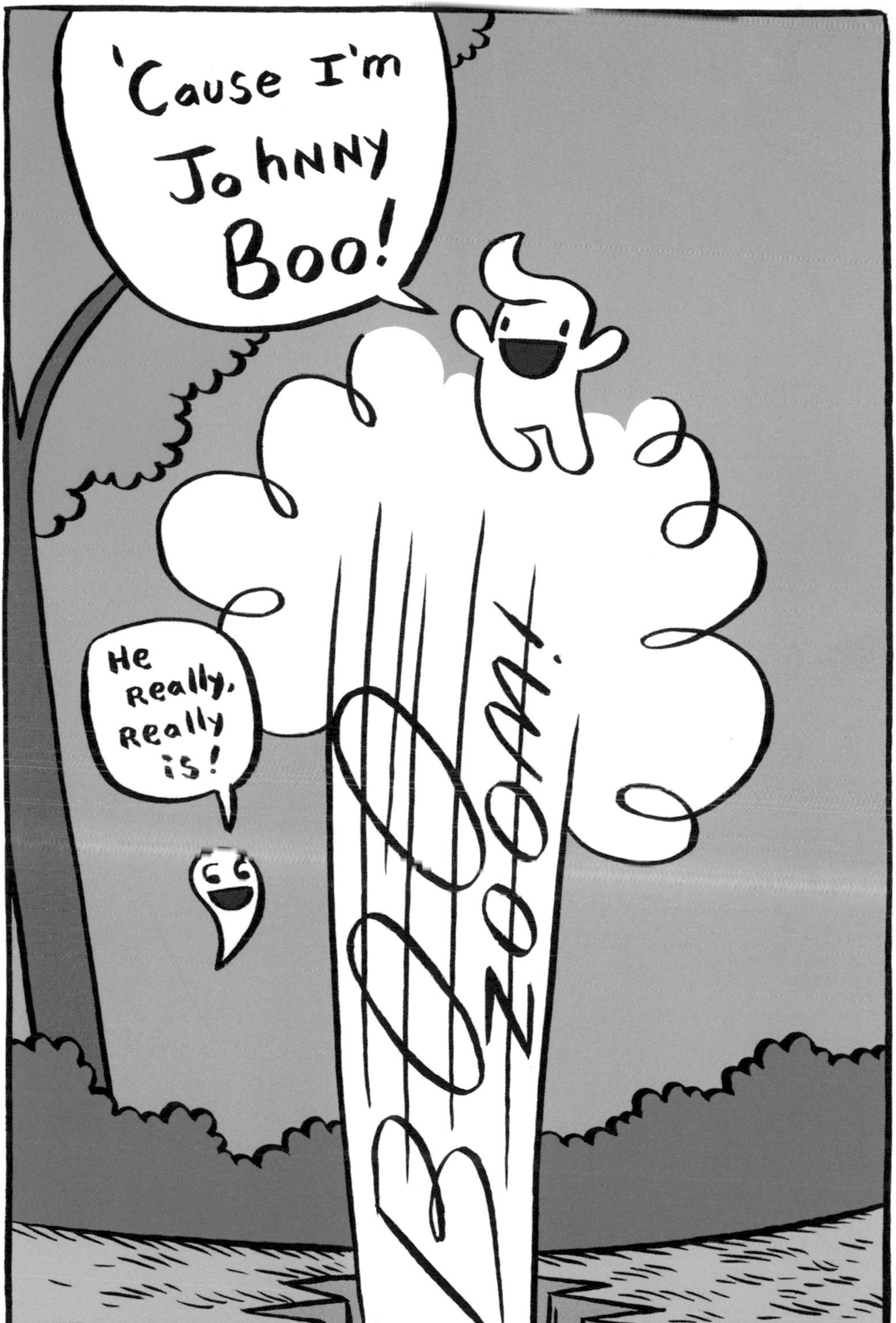
'Cause I'm Johnny Boo!
He Really, Really is!
BOOOOM!
ZOOM!

THE END & HAPPY BIRTHDAY!

Look, Rocky. Bonus stories!

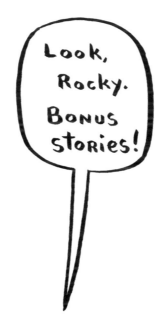

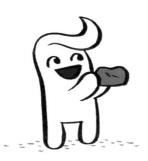

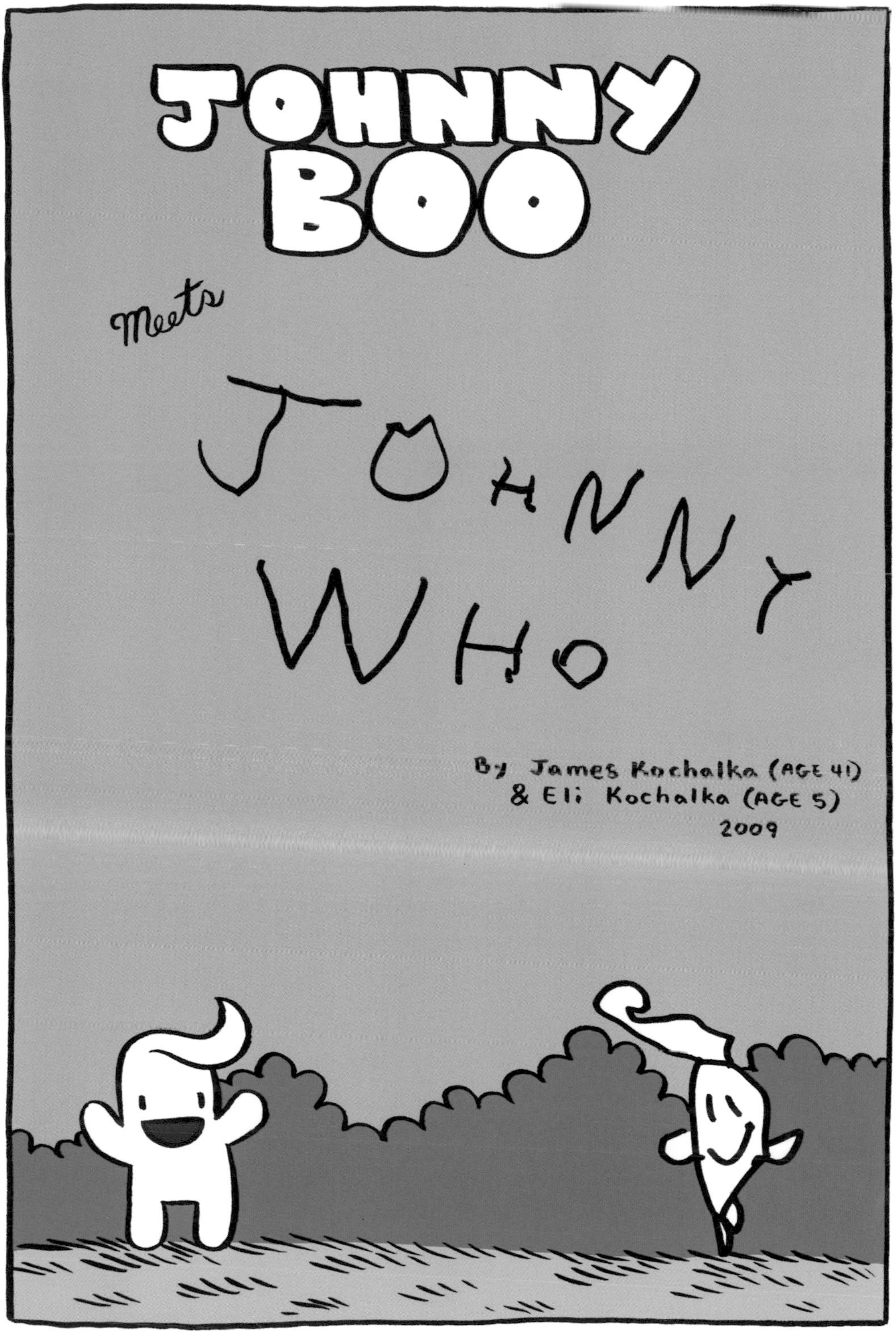
JOHNNY BOO
meets
JOHNNY WHO
By James Kochalka (AGE 41)
& Eli Kochalka (AGE 5)
2009

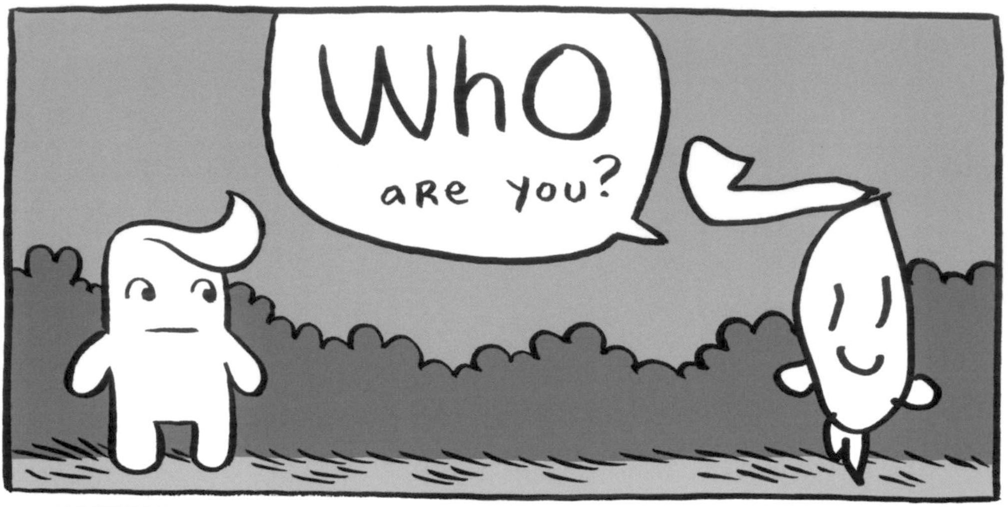
WhO are you?

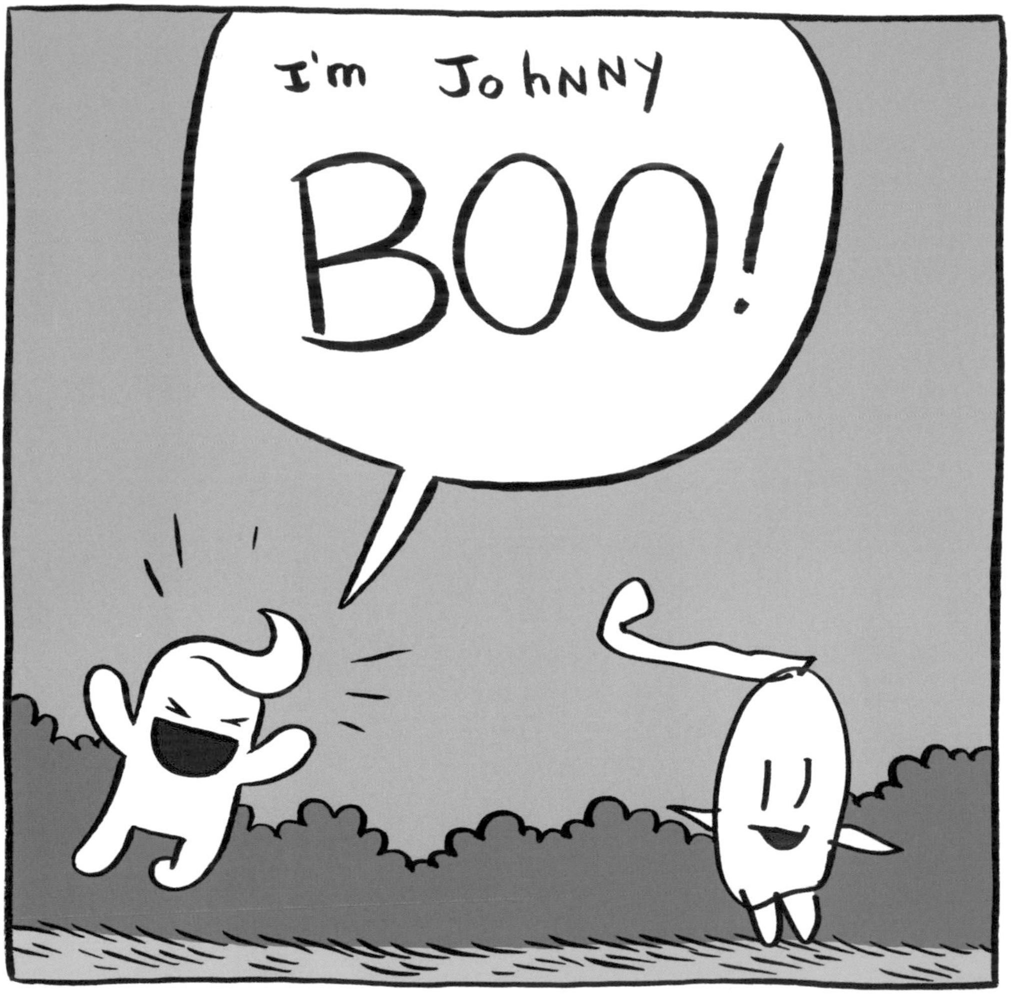
I'm JohNNY BOO!

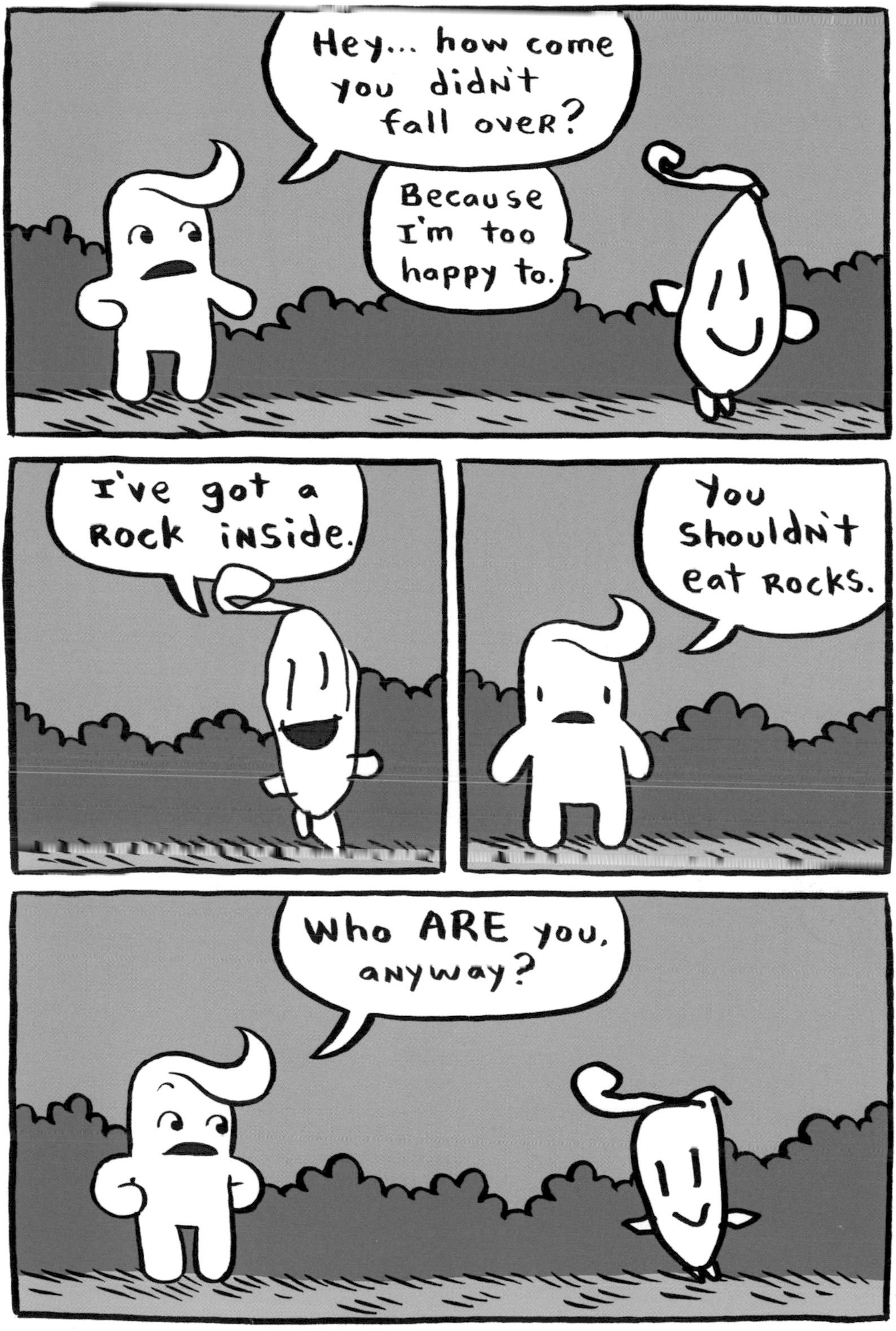
Hey... how come you didn't fall over?
Because I'm too happy to.
I've got a rock inside.
You shouldn't eat rocks.
Who ARE you, anyway?

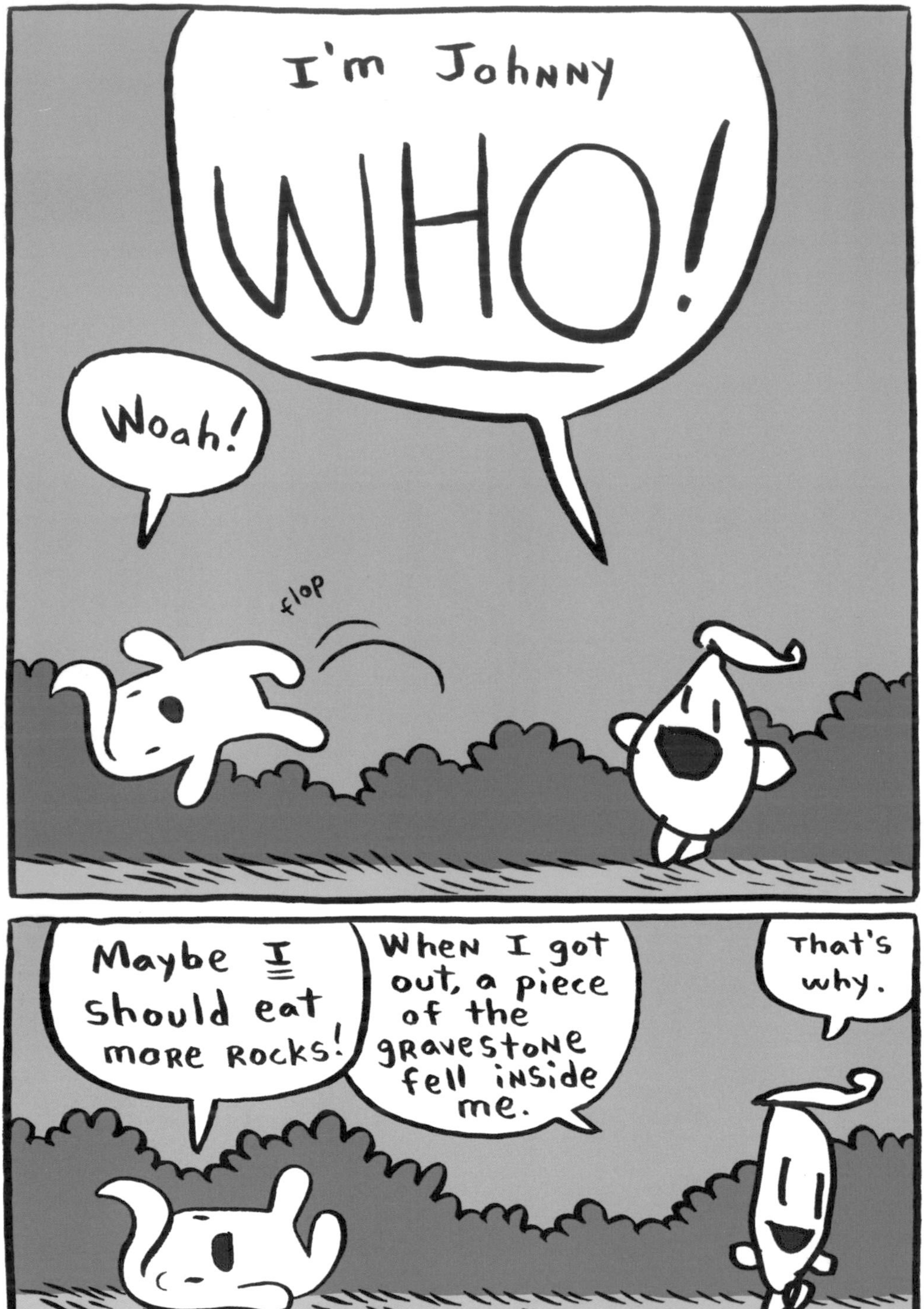
I'm Johnny
WHO!
Woah!
flop
Maybe I should eat more ROCKS!
When I got out, a piece of the gravestone fell inside me.
That's why.

THE END

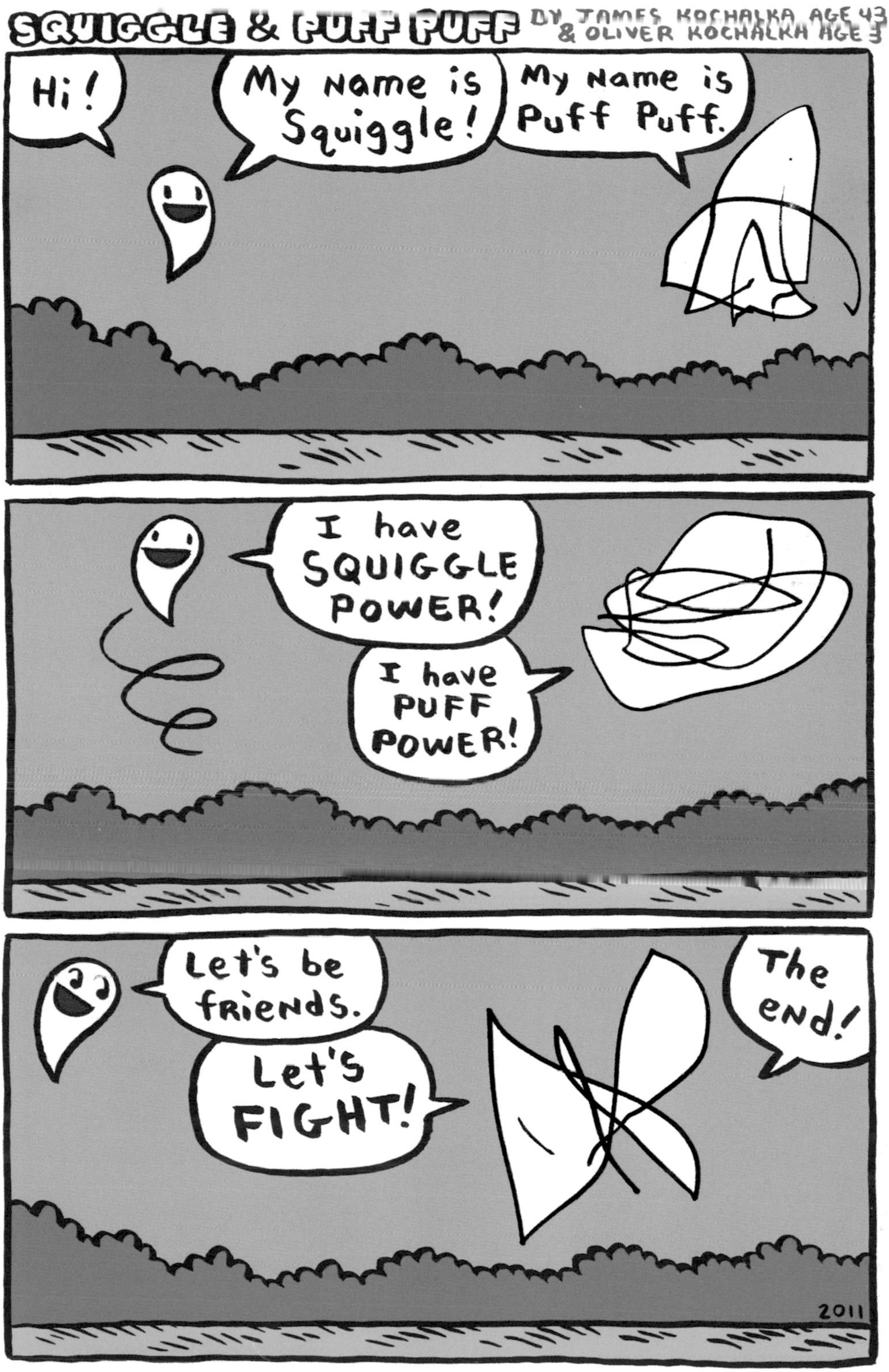
SQUIGGLE & PUFF PUFF
BY JAMES KOCHALKA AGE 43 & OLIVER KOCHALKA AGE 3
Hi!
My name is Squiggle!
My name is Puff Puff.
I have SQUIGGLE POWER!
I have PUFF POWER!
Let's be friends.
Let's FIGHT!
The end!
2011

A PHOTO OF THE AUTHOR: